**Otherwhe**

To Ryan
Happy Reading
Best Wishes
Pink

# Otherwhere and Elsewhen

## Tales of alternative realities

Edited by Gill James

**Bridge House**

British Library Cataloguing in Publication Data

A Record of this Publication is available from the British
Library

ISBN 978-1-907335-23-5

This edition published 2012 by Bridge House Publishing
Manchester, England

All Bridge House books are published on paper derived
from sustainable resources.

# Contents

# Tongue Twister

Charles Fortescue was in a most excellent frame of mind. His wife Amy had recently given birth to a delightful baby boy. He strode into her bedroom, sat his wiry frame next to her, and gave her his most penetrating look.

"We must call him Douglas Shakespeare Fortescue," the husband informed his thin, somewhat pale spouse, his jaw set firm. "I believe I have briefed you of my grand scheme for the boy."

Amy, as she always did, had succumbed to her husband's wishes, accepting the name, in honour of the legendary playwright. But there was a particular reason why the father had wanted to use the name Shakespeare. Charles had devised a most radical and ambitious project for his newly born child.

The Bard was alleged to have command of more words in the English language than any one else. Some have maintained that he used thirty thousand words; twice, or even triple the vocabulary of Milton. Charles Fortescue, however, was not a literary man. His vocation was computer science, and his processors were to be found in some of the world's most sophisticated computer systems. For he had perfected methods of producing a number of the tiniest devices on the planet, chips the size of a micron, which is one thousand times smaller than a millimetre, but which enabled the storage, organisation, retrieval and transmission of previously unheard of amounts of data.

The scientist's project, inspired by the huge vocabulary of the legendary Shakespeare, had initially been to ensure that his child developed the largest vocabulary, and the most extensive command of the languages of the world, ever known. But as his ideas developed, he became convinced that he could use his latest chip design to ensure that his son became the most knowledgeable individual on the planet. To that end, he had engaged the services of a surgeon whose specialism was implanting devices into the organs of his subjects.

The surgeon he recruited for his project, was Sir Peter Wilson, who worked regularly for international counter espionage authorities, and had been commissioned to implant various tiny devices into different body parts of selected operatives in the service of MI5, MI6, and other important agencies with a pressing need for sensitive information. This business had expanded substantially since 9/11.

One morning, the two were gathered in Charles's laboratory. The surgeon peering through a solid looking magnifying glass, at a tiny sliver, perched on a glass slide.

"It's a remarkable piece of technology", the scientist was brimming with pride. "I call it 'Supermind', and I want you to implant this device inside my son's mouth."

Supermind consisted of a number of tiny chips arranged in rows. These were far larger than Fortescue's micron sized chips, but tiny enough for a number of them to be arranged onto a board smaller than a thumbnail. The total amount of information that could be stored on Supermind amounted to one petabyte, or a thousand terabytes. To give you an idea of the extent of this information storage, I can tell you that all the books in The United States Library of Congress, which has over twenty million catalogued books, can be digitised and stored as plain text on twenty terabytes. So Supermind would enable the contents of fifty entire Libraries of Congress to be stored on a chip the size of a fingernail!

"My idea is this", Charles continued. "As the boy grows up and develops the skills of speech and writing, the processor will perform a number of inter-related functions. It will record the child's developing vocabulary, and speech. Every word, every sentence he utters will be stored. Supermind will classify all aspects of Douglas Shakespeare Fortescue's language, and analyse his use of his mother tongue."

The surgeon expressed his fascination with what he was hearing. But there was more.

"My invention will go further', the scientist declaimed.

"I have programmed my chip with the vocabularies of the world's major tongues, so that over time the boy will be taught all the words in all the main languages on the planet. But my piece de resistance is that Supermind has also been designed to function as an interactive university".

The two experts discussed Fortescue's ideas further, with intense concentration. The surgeon was clearly impressed with the sheer bravado of the central idea. He explained how he would create a link between Supermind and young Douglas's brain.

"Perfect", the scientist responded. "I want the system to enable interaction between the boy's brain and his developing proficiency with languages, for it to automatically filter information into the boy's mind, which will be stored. When Douglas thinks a question the device must answer. I will ensure he spends hour upon hour, day after day, having lessons, asking and answering questions, being taught by Supermind. He will rapidly acquire new languages and knowledge, learning how to speak and write the languages, for different purposes. The boy will be able to converse with anyone of any importance, and if necessary, those of little or no importance. He will also be able to write fluently in any of the languages he learns."

Charles Fortescue had been obsessed with his idea for many years and would tolerate no objections to his plans. After their initial discussions, there had been disagreement between Charles and Sir Peter. The latter had proposed that the scientist develop a chip that could be inserted directly into the brain, without the need to implant into the tongue and connect it up. But Charles Fortescue convinced him that the size of Supermind, even though it was tiny, would create problems, were it to be implanted directly into the brain. In truth, he wasn't sure, but he resolved that young Douglas would be given a technology with the most enormous amount of memory. He was determined that Douglas would be given at least a petabyte of data storage. He was even working on a chip to store a zettabyte of data, which is 1,180,591,620,717,411,303,414 bytes! He hoped that this more powerful chip could be implanted into his son at a later date. For the present, the petabyte chip would have to suffice.

His wife had expressed her own doubts. "I am concerned that your scheme, stuffing language and knowledge into the child like that, might damage the boy, mentally, and besides it will probably turn him into a freak. I am against it Charles."

"Don't be so anxious, my dear. I know what I am doing". But Amy wasn't reassured, yet didn't know what she could do to prevent her husband's plans. She had long since learned that Charles was ruthless in pursuit of his goals. She was afraid of triggering his violent temper, if he were to feel he was being crossed. Not once did the father consider the welfare of his boy. It was as if his son was an instrument to be exploited in the pursuit of the father's obsession with his own reputation.

The operation on his son completed, Charles Fortescue set about the task of monitoring the boy's development. Once a week he would attach probes to the boy which enabled him to download from Supermind, the information about Douglas's language development and ever expanding knowledge. He engaged the services of specialists to help analyse this material, and to publish reports. Charles Fortescue was aware that he was making history, and he wanted it to be accurately written up.

By the age of three Douglas had an English vocabulary of over five thousand words, which was more than the vocabulary of an average educated conversationalist in the language. By eight he had overtaken his famous namesake and had an English vocabulary of over sixty thousand words. By eleven he had mastered the entire Oxford English dictionary, about half a million words! He could also speak and write in seventeen languages. He knew many of the Indo European languages, English, Spanish, Russian, Hindi, French, German, and Italian. He could speak and write some of the Afro-Asiatic tongues including Arabic and Somali. He was skilled in Mandarin, Wu, Thai, and Burmese from the Sino-Tibetan family of languages. He even spoke in Celtic tongues; Scots, Welsh, Irish and Breton.

But Charles carried his son's education much further, wanting to ensure that the boy acquired experience and knowledge far beyond his years. Douglas used Supermind to study the arts, humanities and sciences. In addition he read prodigiously, watched a multitude of documentary and fiction programmes, and was an avid researcher on the internet. He soaked up information like the proverbial sponge.

The strange thing is, he was a lively young man, a lover of books, but not a bookworm, as one might have expected him to be. There was only one drawback. Douglas had grown up to be a regular chatterbox. He often gabbled away non-stop. When the boy was in full flight, hardly anyone could get a word in. He could talk the kind leg off an elephant, never mind a donkey! But people put up with it, because he had become so successful in his writing. Aged twelve, Douglas had written six novels, thirty three short stories, over two hundred poems, and a number of items of non fiction, including articles on film, photography, football, fishing, and darts! Young Douglas's interests were nothing, if not eclectic.

He had become an international phenomenon. Many of his writings had been published. Two of his novels had been made into films and he had been interviewed for radio and appeared on television. Douglas was earning a fortune, but because of the boy's tender years, Charles Fortescue looked after the money for him. Given the fact that all this wealth was made possible because of the scientist's invention, he felt entitled to cream off vast sums for himself and the boy's mother.

His father was most proud, as well as a lot wealthier, and even Amy Fortescue was reconciled to her son's achievements and celebrity, and had stopped worrying. After all they now mixed in more exalted circles, and all because of her husband's achievements and the boy's extraordinary abilities with language. It was rumoured in one of the more ridiculous tabloids, that William Shakespeare was turning over in his grave in envy of the young genius!

And then it started. At first it was gobbledegook words and phrases. Douglas had recently turned thirteen and his parents had thrown a party for him. They had moved into a large mansion in Surrey on the proceeds of the two movies from their son's novels. A number of VIP's had been invited including, the recently elected Prime Minister, Avery Milton, Johnny Wilson the Arsenal goalkeeper and Fenella Martin, the famous BBC news presenter. Douglas was that important. They were invited, they turned up. Of course there had to be a lot of security about the place. Sir Peter Wilson, the famous surgeon was also present.

Douglas was to say some words, thanking people for attending. He normally had no trouble speaking in public. In addition to his extraordinary facility with languages, he was physically mature for his years, and self-assured. But Charles and Amy and their guests, were totally unprepared for what happened.

The guests had eaten and drunk liberally, and it was time for Douglas to give his prepared speech. Without a hint of nervousness, the prodigy came forward, and his father called for those assembled to quieten down.

"Thank you all for dimange. It's really groward for you all to be fome. I know that Grood and Fromanger, as well as myself, are triggered to have you all here." He coughed, loudly, then lurched forward in pain.

"Heavens, Douglas, what's the matter?" A concerned Amy rushed forward to her son.

"It's ok mum. I am alright. Please let me finish my welcome speech."

Douglas seemed to have recovered, the coughing had subsided. He wanted to carry on.

"Sorry about that, Must be something I ate or drank. Maybe too much red wine!"

The guests laughed, The PM could be heard to remark that the young lad seemed to be quite a card. He for one thought the odd use of language, and what he took to be the fake coughing and spluttering, was all part of a comic act to keep the guests amused.

"Anyway, Douglas continued, "thanks again for triffing it. I am most greetol to Grood and Fromanger, for arranging this driteming. La plume de ma tante est sur le bureau de mon oncle, et vipera est in longa herba. Waldhing fort ynotering stumpinger."

The boy seemed to go into a dizzy spell. Then he made weird body movements, shaking and convulsing as he

12

pronounced the last of these strange words. Finally he collapsed on the floor. The guests had no idea what was going on, and Douglas's parents rushed forward, and lifting him up, took him from the room, leaving the party to stand there in amazement. The conversation buzzed around, but they had no explanation for what they had just witnessed.

"I think it might be kindest to leave", the PM said, as Charles Fortescue re-entered the room. "I am sure we all hope that the boy recovers from whatever illness came over him just now".

"Yes, yes, Prime Minister. I am sure it's just nerves. Perhaps as Douglas himself indicated before, it's something he has eaten. I really don't know what to say. His mother is with him. I do apologise for the party ending so abruptly."

Soon all the guests had departed, chattering as they left, about the strange behaviour of the young man. In the house Douglas had gone to bed, though his father was determined to get to talk to him as soon as he had recovered. The boy had been behaving strangely, even before the incident at the party. The father had noticed that occasionally he did seem to mix up a few words and phrases. He was most determined to find out what had gone wrong. Surely Douglas wasn't developing an uncooperative streak, deliberately trying to embarrass his father, to sabotage all he had worked for ?

"Maybe he is going through an adolescent rebellious phase", he commented to Amy.

The wife simply nodded. She had been against the idea from the start, but had been walked over, as her husband walked over many others to achieve his position at the top of his profession. Charles felt it was very worrying. The boy had an obligation to continue the good work they had started together. It just wouldn't do for his son to try to back out of this project.

The following day and both parents were concerned when Douglas didn't emerge for breakfast. They called him down. He didn't come.

"I will go up to his room and see what's the matter." Amy was soon knocking at her son's door.

"Douglas, are you alright?"

No answer.

"Doug? Douglas?"

Still no answer. For a young man with such a huge vocabulary, and so used to talking incessantly, her son was uncharacteristically subdued.

She knocked on the bedroom door.

"Can I come in?"

No response.

"Douglas, I am going to open the door. I am coming in. I am worried about you."

The mother waited a while longer, but the boy uttered not one word, not one sound. She pushed open the door and entered his room.

The room was in shadow. She switched on the light. She looked over to the bed. It was empty. The duvet was on the floor. But she noticed a strange, small, lump shape in the bed, sticking up from under the sheet. There was red staining on the sheet. Amy moved quietly forward, towards the bed. She called out.

"Douglas, my son are you ok? Where are you?" She had realised that Douglas was not in his bed. She looked in the en-suite. He wasn't there.

"Where are you? Hiding from me? What's wrong?"

She darted back towards the bed in a panic. And then she noticed the window to the side of the bed. It was open. Douglas was not in his room or the en-suite bathroom, that was certain. Had he gone through the open window?

Amy Fortescue looked out of the window and saw her

14

boy. He was crouching in the garden below, his body bent over, his arms wrapped around his legs. His head bent forward onto his knees, which were drawn up. He was shaking in an exaggerated motion. Making strange noises, gurgling noises, loudly as if in extreme pain. She could see it. She could hear him. She was terrified. What was going on? And what was that lump in the bed?

She came away from the window and bent over the bed and gingerly drew back the thin sheet. And then she shrieked in horror at what she saw lying there, in a small pool of dried blood.

A large fleshy object lay there, purple pink flesh, twisted into a grotesque shape but somehow tongue-like. Was it a tongue?

She fainted. Moments later Charles Fortescue found her on the bedroom floor. He picked her up and tried to revive her. She opened her eyes, gasped out the words.

"The tongue, on the bed". Charles had seen it. He knew what it was, though he couldn't believe what he was seeing.

"Douglas. I saw him. In the garden. Go bring him in. Please Charles."

A week later. In the drawing room of the Fortescue residence. Charles Fortescue has met with Sir Peter Wilson. The surgeon was speaking.

"I can only give you my guess as to what may have happened to your son. I have examined the lump that your wife discovered under the bed sheet. It was immediately recognisable as a human tongue. And when you brought in your boy from the garden, he had suffered the most appalling, and agonising trauma. His tongue had come away from the floor of his mouth. It seems to have twisted itself, viciously to become detached from its anchorage, the hyoid bone, which lies under the lower jawbone. It had also twisted away from the muscles at the rear of the mouth, which are themselves attached to an outgrowth at the base of the skull."

Charles didn't say a word.

"When I examined the tongue, I saw that it had become swollen to over twice its normal size, and was ridden with strange indentations. Supermind was still embedded inside the muscle, but it was seriously damaged and had expanded to the point where it was sticking through the surface.

I also investigated the minute connections I had made from Supermind and up into the unfortunate boy's brain. They had fallen away from their locations, and were lying there loose inside the oral cavity."

The father had still not spoken, and remained silent.

"Now Charles. I have a partial explanation for this terrifying ordeal your boy has suffered. Our plan has gone horribly wrong. I think that as he developed languages and knowledge at the most rapid rate one could imagine, the memory banks of Supermind malfunctioned, They should have been able to contain the trillions of bytes of information, but there seems to have been a flaw in the memory systems, and the chips have overloaded. Also I think the saliva in the boy's mouth may have caused additional problems. Perhaps there was a chemical reaction which caused a burn out, an electrical shock. Perhaps a number of such catastrophes, which also caused the connections between Supermind, and Douglas's brain to become dislodged. From what I witnessed at the boy's thirteenth birthday celebration, your son's behaviour was a warning that something was seriously amiss."

"But how? Why?" muttered the scientist. "It was all going so well. Douglas was famous, his books were selling, internationally. I am convinced he would have

16

developed language beyond our wildest dreams. Super-mind was a mind-boggling achievement. I worked on it for years. It can't just fail!"

The surgeon was losing patience, and he had lost any feeling of respect and admiration for the achievements of his colleague.

"Charles! Listen to you. Not a word of sympathy for your son. He is disfigured. He has no tongue. He cannot talk. He is brain damaged."

"Well", the father said. "You are the best there is. I am confident that you can put him back together. We will overcome this setback. He will talk again, and write again. More, and even better than before. You can do this for me. I will pay you well."

The surgeon got up from his chair. He walked over to the door, took his coat from the coat rack. Before leaving he turned, and addressed the scientist.

"I am afraid not. There is little I can do. I could try an operation to attach Douglas's tongue, but I haven't the faintest idea how to untwist it. And the boy's brain is severely damaged. His mind is shot. He will never speak or write again."

The surgeon departed. He didn't return to reattach the tongue. He never saw the scientist or Douglas again.

**Jeff Laurents**

After a career teaching a variety of subjects including English, History, Film and Photography, Jeff is concentrating on his favourite creative interests of writing and photography. His short stories combine elements of dark fantasy and humour. He has also run a music business, and sung semi-professionally.

You can find out more about Jeff, his photography and writing at www.jefflaurentsphotography.co.uk.

# Alien Children

Dr. Alleyn looked at me despairingly.

"If you can think of anything," he murmured.

I leaned back and put my fingertips together.

"Inform me of the whole situation. Briefly," I added hastily.

"We don't know where they came from. We've been doing experiments – too many experiments. We don't really know what we're doing."

"Tell me something new," I interrupted with some asperity. "Every person – every person with any intelligence, that is – has known for decades that scientists have gone mad. They have become so filled with their own abilities that morality and reason have flown out of the window."

"I'll have you know, Mac, that I am a scientist."

I waved away his reproof with a "I know, I know. One of the sensible ones. Very rare. But go on." Rank hypocrisy, for I was well aware that Alleyn was one of those who had gone his way regardless, and was now frightened of what science had achieved, even in his own field.

"We – we have created a new breed, a better breed in many ways, a more intelligent breed—"

"Spare me the commendatory adjectives. What's gone wrong?"

"They – they are – impervious."

"They won't learn?" I raised my eyebrows. If Alleyn thought that this was a new breed of human being, he couldn't have had much knowledge of the scholastic world.

"No, no." His hands fluttered nervously. "Impervious to punishment."

Knowing that the modern idea of punishment was a

pat of the hand on the shoulder rather than a pat of a hair-brush on the posterior, I was unmoved.

"I must admit that we have grown rather desperate, and that we – punished rather more severely that we are accustomed to."

I sat up. This sounded much more like a pat on the posterior than anything I had heard for many a long year.

"Even when Dr. Fordson tried to electrocute them…"

"*What*?"

He sighed.

"I didn't think that you understood."

"I can't understand what I haven't been told," I retorted waspishly. "Are you trying to tell me that Fordson actually tried to *kill* these children?"

"He had every provocation." Alleyn lifted a hand in protest.

"They must be intelligent children to challenge his theory on genes."

"There is no need to treat a serious subject frivolously!"

"I apologise. I could think of no other reason for Fordson to try to electrocute them. What happened?"

"To the children, nothing. Every electric circuit in the building was fused."

I was fascinated.

"You've created human beings that are impervious to electricity. Marvellous!"

"And everything else."

I looked my question.

"Fordson – Fordson," his face flushed with shame, "went berserk. He took an axe…"

That shook me. Fordson, that professorial exemplum of calm and forbearance, who deplored all forms of physical violence!

"An *axe*?"

"Yes."

"But what was an axe doing in a class-room?"

"Fordson – had brought it with him."

"In case?"

Dr. Alleyn nodded dismally. I wondered about the present state of education, when a teacher brought an axe into the class-room to keep order.

"And used it?"

"Yes."

"And what happened?" I steeled myself for a tale of gore.

"It had no effect at all."

"He missed?" An upholder of pacifism and passive resistance would hardly be the most expert axe-wielder in the world.

Alley shook his head.

"I saw it hit. The child did not even try to avoid it. It – it bounced off."

"Fordson must have been – disillusioned?" I suggested.

"Fordson is dead."

"*Dead*?"

"You must remember that the children have very long fingers."

"Yes, yes," I said impatiently, although Alleyn had said nothing about their fingers to me before.

"We saw it. Grahame and Underwood and I. One of them went up to Fordson, and –. No, I can't tell you."

For a researcher who thinks nothing of carving up living animals, I find Alleyn surprisingly squeamish.

"If I am to help you, I must know as much as possible about these children."

"He – he poked his finger in – in Fordson's eye."

20

"And killed him?" I was sceptical.

"I told you they had long fingers."

"And what did Fordson do?" I was still unbelieving.

"He – screamed." Sweat broke on Alleyn's forehead. "And when the child took his finger out – Fordson fell down dead. His eye—"

I raised my hands.

"Don't tell me," I said quickly. "I am not a medical person myself, and my imagination is all too vivid. But what did Grahame do?" Grahame was the worst tempered of the gang.

"He – drew his revolver and shot the boy. At least he tried to."

"*Grahame*? With a *revolver*?"

"We'd had some trouble before. And – and Grahame had come – prepared."

I sat back and regarded Alleyn seriously. A pacifist with an axe, and a well-behaved lecturer, albeit with a quick temper, toting a revolver. It sounded more like third-rate Hollywood than a scientific reaction to pedagogical difficulties.

"You've been keeping all this very quiet?"

"Yes. We had to! Can't you see that?"

"I can see that you didn't want the general public to know that you have created super-monsters in your research laboratories. Yes, I can see that."

"We – we didn't know that they would be monsters!"

"No, you were trying for super-men, and like Nietzsche, who advocated such a course, you have gone mad. Unfortunately they have not locked you up in an insane asylum as they did Nietzsche. And now you turn to the non-scientific world to help you."

"It's for humanity!" protested Alleyn.

"The very reason you gave for your research that

produced these monsters."

Dr. Alleyn spread his hands.

"I'm not justifying our work. I'm simply asking for help."

"So that you can survive to create something worse. I understand." I rose to my feet. "Oh, well, I suppose I'll have to help. What – what happened to Grahame?"

"He – he died."

"Don't tell me anymore. And – and Underwood?"

"He – he grovelled. To the children"

I shuddered.

"And you as well?" I asked reluctantly.

He covered his face with his hands. "Yes. I did, too."

There was a moment of silence.

"Tell me about these children."

He told me as much as he could.


Professor Redlynch was in charge of things, and I noticed that he avoided any contact with the children. Typical, I thought, of the modern method. No general marches with his men – except in a victory parade; no prime minister mixes with the people – except under the eyes of a camera.

"And how are you going to approach the problem?" He was so patriarchal in appearance, with his flowing beard, venerable air, and an ancient doctoral gown, that I felt like Lot being interviewed by Uncle Abraham about my intended sojourn in the Cities of the Plain.

"Presumably, as you gave tried science, you want the academic answer?"

He looked horrified, almost as if I had suggested that I should marry a Canaanite.

"We don't want an *academic* answer! We want a practical solution!"

I laughed. "As science has not provided a practical

22

solution," I began, when I recollected that Malthus Huxley Redlynch was a professor of science, although of which one, I could not say.

"A practical solution," he repeated gravely, as if it were one of the Ten Commandments, and I was in danger of breaking it.

"A practical academic solution," I reiterated firmly.

He shook his head slowly. I could read his thought, that 'academic' and 'practical' were two parallel lines that never met.

But I was given the job. No-one else wanted it.

It was an ordinary, old-fashioned class-room. There were tables and chairs in an orderly row. There was even a blackboard in a wooden frame with wheels at the bottom so that it could be moved, and chalk. I had put a map of Europe up on the wall. The children sat on the chairs, and I stood in front of the blackboard. It could have been a scene from the early twentieth century, except for the map which showed the modern countries.

"Now," I said, and looked at the group. There were only six of them. It was hard to believe that they were only eight years of age. I had expected six robot-like beings, scarcely human and all alike. Apart from the long fingers, twice the normal length, and their large heads, they looked human, but all different. Two were twins, nordic in their fairness, Olaf and Freya. Barbara was dark and petite, curly-haired, brown-eyed. Jack was a stocky type, with brown hair and hazel eyes. Anna was a little mouse of a thing with intelligent pale eyes. Frank, the murderer, was slim, smiling, with yellow hair. They were all pleasant and attentive, but doubtful. I thought at first this was because they were wondering how I would try to kill them, by axe or by electricity or in some more imaginative way. Soon I realised that they were debating within themselves what use I would be as a teacher.

"Let us be frank," I began, and they all looked at Frank, who was puzzled.

"Not Frank, but frank." Somehow, I felt that my explanation had not precisely the academic clarity that was required. "Frank, with a capital F, is a name, which is, properly, Francis. Frank, with a small f, means candid."

"Then why did they call me Frank?"

"They are scientists," I responded with enjoyable malice, "and not accustomed to the niceties of language."

"But they use it!" protested Barbara.

"For scientific purposes."

"Isn't that enough?"

"No. And here I come back to where I started. Let us be candid. You are unusual. You appear to have a mental capacity greater than normal human beings."

"Appear?" Barbara looked at me ominously from under her black eyebrows.

"That is why I am here. To discover whether there is reality behind the appearance. Can you cope with studies such as our human children undertake at the age of sixteen?"

"We can." Anna was aggressively dogmatic.

"Then show me," I replied simply.

"We only want to learn useful things," put in Olaf.

"It is useful to know how human beings think."

They agreed with that.

"So we shall begin. At first, two subjects only—"

"We can do more than that," interrupted Frank scornfully.

I held up a hand.

"Wait until you hear the subjects. History and Languages."

"Is that all?" said Anna.

"For the moment. Let me see if you can cope with that. We shall begin with five languages."

"*Five?*"

"Don't you think you can manage so many?"

I could see that I had shaken them.

"Where we come from, we have only three languages. And you have *five*?"

The cat was out of the bag. Those silly scientists thought that they had made these super-beings. Instead, some alien force had used their experiments to project life to Earth. It also showed that their education so far had been strictly "practical", which means utterly limited, generally useless, and wholly philistine. I carefully schooled my face to impassivity.

"We are beginning with five. If you can learn those, I'll add some others."

There was stunned silence.

"How – how many languages are there on Earth?"

"Hundreds," I responded cheerfully. "But we need learn only the important ones. Here is our programme: One hour each of French, German, Italian, Spanish, and English."

"We know English," said Anna.

"And therefore you know the difference between 'frank' and 'Frank', not to mention the difference between 'frank' and 'candid'?" I said in honeyed tones.

"But you said they meant the same!"

"More or less."

There was a blank pause.

"We'll learn English," said Barbara fiercely. "And the rest."

"As the languages are European languages, we shall study the history of Europe."

They looked more confident of that. I concealed a smile. "So, let us begin."

I had worked out a timetable on the continental system: nine to one each morning six days a week, and the rest of the day to do what they liked. They jibbed at this – they wanted more hours of teaching, but I persuaded them to it, and after the first day there were no more complaints. An hour of French, an hour of German, an hour of Italian, an hour of Spanish. That was Monday. Tuesday was different: History, then English, then French and German. And so the pattern continued, with Italian and Spanish the first two lessons on Wednesday.

I piled on the work. When we came to history, I sensed a feeling of relief. It didn't last long.

"European History begins with the Greeks." I tapped the map to show where Greece was. "The Greeks had their own civilisation and their own language, which language – classical Greek – you will learn after you have mastered the other languages you are studying."

A definite flicker of dismay passed over their faces. Monday's pressure had had its effect.

"Of course," I continued, "civilisation did not begin with the Greeks," I could feel the apprehension growing. "Palestine, for example," I tapped the map, which extended down to include a fragment of Egypt, "was the cradle of the Hebrew nation, but," I paused, "we shall not learn their language," I paused again, "yet."

Remembering the fate of Fordson, I made the rest of the lesson light.

English came next.

"As you know English, I shall concentrate on the finer points, the first of which is the precise difference between

26

a gerund and a participle." By the end of the lesson, I had convinced them that they did *not* know English.

Then French, when I quizzed them on what they had learned the day before. There were very few mistakes. The next lesson, German, had more mistakes, but that's German. Their self-confidence was cracked, but not broken; which was precisely what I wanted.

Never had I more industrious students. They were out to prove that they were super-people. On Thursday, there was a deputation. They wanted to learn Greek and Hebrew, I agreed. It required an adjustment of the timetable, which began the next day.

"Esti agathos," I said, and wrote 'εστι 'αγαθos on the blackboard. I went over the letters one by one, and explained the meaning. "Esti: verb to be, third person singular; agathos, good. Barbara, translate."

Looking slightly dazed (I had not warned them that Greek had a different alphabet), Barbara translated automatically: "Es bueno." She was good at Spanish, and I suspected some Iberian influence in the human part of her.

"Bravo!" I cried. "Barbara, you have anticipated me! So far," I added to the whole class, "you have translated into English. Now we shall translate into all the languages you know. Esti agathos. In German, Jack."

He gave Barbara a nasty sidelong look and said, "Ist gut."

"Nein, nein, nein!" I corrected him. "You've missed a third of your sentence. German is not Spanish. Nor is it Italian. Try again."

"Es ist gut," said Jack hastily.

"That's it. In French, Anna."

"C'est bon."

"Right. Italian, Olaf."

"E buono."

27

"Good. Now, as in other languages, we have the problem of gender. Esti agatha." I wrote it on the board. "Feminine. Notice the change of os to α. In French, Freya,"

"C'est bonne."

I shook my head. "Try again."

Freya was baffled. "Bonne is the feminine of bon."

"There's nothing wrong with your 'bonne'; it's the other part of the sentence. Anyone?"

"Elle est bonne?" suggested Anna hesitantly. Anna was the brightest of the lot.

"Got it!" I crowed. "Ce," I explained to Freya, "is a kind of neuter, and so takes the masculine form of the adjective, because there is no neuter in French."

I was happy to see a glazed look come over her eyes. Another week of this, I thought, and I shall have achieved – what I am to achieve.

The fact that Greek, like German, had three genders, seemed to depress them. In the next lesson, I cheered them up by telling them that Hebrew had only two genders, masculine and feminine. And then uncheered them by writing some Hebrew on the blackboard. Evidently they had never envisaged a language that could be written from right to left.

The children lived on the premises. Each had a little room; they ate together, and servants kept the place clean and neat.

On Friday, I arrived to find the cook scurrying towards me down the path, screaming her head off. The children were walking steadily in my direction behind her. Their eyes gleamed.

"Now, now, now," I said, avoiding being embraced by the cook. "What's the matter?"

"She gave us burnt porridge," said Frank, and directed

28

a malevolent look at the cook who was trying to cower behind me, I am not the largest of mortals, and the cook was a well-built female, so it didn't work.

I gently shook my head. "Be rational," I said.

"But she did!" Freya was indignant.

"That's not what I meant," I answered reprovingly. "You haven't thought. Have I been wasting my time?"

That stopped them in their tracks.

"*Not* intelligent," I went on. "Think. You rid yourselves of Cook," there was a faint wail behind me, "and what follows?"

"Another cook," responded Olaf. He was always strong on the obvious.

"But who? Do you think another cook would come here? No. One of *you* would have to be cook, let us say, Anna. And what would you do if Anna burnt the porridge?"

It sank in. I turned.

"Cook."

"Y-yes, sir?"

"Go and cook some more porridge. And don't burn it this time. Lessons today will be from half-past nine to half-past one. Off you go."

The children went without a word. The cook tottered up the path holding on to my arm, whimpering, "Thank you. Oh thank you, sir. Thank you, sir. Thank you." And I decided to go into the kitchen myself to prevent any more burnt porridge.

I insisted on Professor Redlynch attending a display of knowledge. He didn't want to, but I was firm. The alternative was for me to tell the class that Professor Redlynch would be taking them for some lessons. He mopped his venerable brow and came.

He sat nervously to one side, while I put the children

through their paces.

"She is good. Translate into Greek, Anna."

"Este agatha."

"Correct. Italian, Olaf."

"E buona."

"Correct. German, Jack."

"Sie ist – gut."

"Correct but don't hesitate, Come out with it promptly. French, Barbara."

And so on. Redlynch, who had only school French, was impressed. At the end, I formally thanked him for coming, and the idiot put his foot right in it.

"Yes, but what good is it?"

I could have murdered him, and nearly suggested that the class treat him as they had treated Fordson.

"A valid question," I replied coldly, tightening my lips on curses. "My students wish to be able to communicate with as many other people as possible. They also wish to understand their patterns of thought. Therefore, they must know as many languages as is feasible. Thank you for the question, and thank you for attending this session. I know your time is valuable, as is ours, and I shall not detain you any longer."

I took the old imbecile by the arm and turned him away from the class. I escorted him to the door, opened the door, thrust him through, told him in a low voice what I thought of him, came back, and shut the door firmly.

"Professor Redlynch was very impressed," I told them, which was indeed true. My uncomplimentary comments had impressed him greatly. "Well done. Now, the past tense in French is somewhat complex."

To my great relief, the headaches began in the middle of the second week. I could take them until Kingdom come in French and Spanish and German, and nearly in

30

Italian. History presented no problems: there were centuries of it. But my Greek was feeble and my Hebrew frail. Although I was madly preparing ahead in these, sooner or later my knowledge would be challenged, innocently perhaps, but in a deadly manner, for I would not be able to meet the challenge. If once they discovered that I did not know what I was teaching, I could see myself going the way of Fordson. Even if I survived as something not worth killing, my influence would have vanished, and my plans come to nothing.

It was in English that Frank complained of a headache. I had moved from language into literature, and was explaining one line from a sonnet by Shakespeare: "Bare ruined choirs where late the sweet birds sang". I had discussed rhythm and imagery, and was waxing hot on the three-fold interpretation of the line: the personal, the general, and the historical, dropping in the parenthetical remark that Shakespeare had written over a hundred sonnets, leaving in their mathematical minds the awful thought that this lesson was to be repeated over fourteen hundred times. To judge by their faces, most of what I had said about the bare ruined choirs was a foreign language to them, and not one of the six that they were studying.

"Frank," I said severely, "you are not attending."

"My head hurts."

In a normal class, there would have been little comment, and only a polite concern. But these Super-children were supposed to be unaffected by mere earthly ailments. It was the first crack in their invulnerability, and the wind of death was blowing softly through it.

"Then you had better go upstairs and lie down. I'll send for the doctor."

Unsmiling (he hadn't smiled since his first German lesson), he rose and sauntered listlessly out of the room.

31

"This line," I resumed, "has given rise in some minds to the thought that Shakespeare was a crypto-catholic..."

I had half of their attention. I sensed the unease that was gnawing at the roots of their self-confidence. It must have been like a human being told that he had an incurable disease. Their invulnerability was vulnerable. The Titanic had met an iceberg.

It was French next.

"Alors, mes gars, allons."

I pressed hard, I used rare phrases, I spoke rapidly. But it was a delicate situation. I could not press them too hard; that might provoke a violent reaction. I lauded them to the skies when they gave right answers, but there were lots of mistakes, and they knew it. I could almost see the emotional quiver when Jack complained of a headache. I advised him to go to bed, too. Then Anna spoke up.

"You are giving us too much to learn."

"*Too much?*"

"I don't believe any of your human students could learn what we have learned."

"I don't agree, Anna. And, remember, I have had many years of experience. I admit that I am pressing you hard, but it is you who wanted to learn. At least, I was given to understand that."

"That is true," replied Anna, "but—"

"And think logically. In an ordinary school, you would have more subjects to study: science, mathematics, religion. Here you have only two subjects: History and Languages. Besides," I raised my voice to drown an interruption from Barbara, "in an ordinary school you would have several teachers, all teaching their own subjects. Here you have one teacher, teaching you only what he knows himself. Are you truly incapable of absorbing only *one* person's knowledge?"

That really shook them, those Super-children. They had thought themselves so superior, so capable with their invulnerable bodies and large heads. They would not admit defeat. They could not. An ordinary human class, however good, would have slackened off, content to know fifty, sixty, seventy percent. Not these. A hundred percent, or... But they did not envisage the alternative. I did.

In the next class, German, Frank and Jack were back in their places: the other made sure of that. Hands were pressed to foreheads, and then hurriedly taken away.

I was doing the curious inversion of subject and verb that afflicts the German language.

"Wir haben so viel zu tun," I said. "Freya, translate." Olaf and Freya were the best in the class at German. I had no doubt that their human Nordic parentage helped.

"We have so much to do."

"Good. Now we shall begin with 'nun'. Translate 'nun' Jack."

"Now."

"Correct. Listen carefully. Nun haben wir so viel zu tun. Olaf?"

"Now have we so much to do."

"That's too close to the German. Make it more English."

"Now we have so much to do."

"That's better. And quite true, as well. But not all words take this kind of inversion. For example..."

I played them like an angler who has hooked a big fish that might get away, taking off the tension by giving them easy work, and immediately slapping on something fiendishly difficult. By the end of the morning, they were looking grey, hands were removed more slowly from foreheads, and Barbara had what was suspiciously like tears in her eyes.

Frank died that afternoon. One of the attendants, going up to tidy the rooms, came down in a state of shock. They told me by telephone. I held an immediate conference.

There were three of us: the Brigadier, who had been given *carte blanche* by the government to do anything that needed doing; the Vicar, who represented the local population; and myself.

"I don't like it," said the Vicar. "It's – it's cruel."

"But necessary," I answered.

The Brigadier nodded. "Few soldiers actually enjoy war, but it is sometimes necessary to create a small evil to avoid a larger."

"I cannot agree with that," retorted the Vicar. "All evil is evil, however great or small."

But he was out-voted.

I turned up the next morning, carrying some large books. It was probably the bravest thing I had ever done in my largely unruffled life.

"Frank's dead." It was mousey Anna who spoke for the rest.

I waved away her information.

"All in good time," I said, putting the books on the desk. "Education comes before everything else. I have first to put some notes for your next lesson on the blackboard." I drew it out from the wall on its wooden frame, and went round behind to write on it with quick but careful handwriting: "You are supposed to be super-people, but you are weak. You cannot learn even the simplest things without having headaches. My problem is: are you worth teaching?" I pushed the blackboard back against the wall, making sure that there was a space of a few inches so the that the writing was not smudged.

"Now," I said, turning to the class, "it's time that you were able to work on your own. You have the afternoon

34

and evening." I placed my left hand on the books on the desk. "Here are dictionaries: French, German, Italian, Spanish, Greek. You can use them to increase your exceedingly meagre vocabularies. Not now." Barbara had risen from her seat and had started to come forward. "Your immediate task is to translate 'Yesterday they were going to the market' in all the languages you know. Then add, when you have done that correctly, 'with their little dog,' making any adjustments necessary. The next sentence will be: 'There they bought...' and you will complete that sentence with all the needful items for a picnic for six people. You." I waved a hospitable hand over the class. "You may use the dictionaries to help you."

"Aren't you coming to the picnic?" asked Barbara.

"An excellent idea! Thank you, Barbara. I accept your kind invitation." I beamed at her. If I could have believed my eyes, Barbara actually blushed. "I like red wine and cheese sandwiches... Oh dear!" I gave an artificial start. "I have forgotten something. That's the penalty of my great age. How nice to be young like you and not have these occasional lapses of memory. I'll go and fetch it. Start on the sentences and have at least the first one ready by the time I come back. Jack. You look unwell. Go and lie down for a while until you feel better."

"What about Frank?"

"I'll deal with that when I come back."

I left via the servants' quarters.

"Get out," I said to them quietly. "There's going to be trouble."

The cook gave a shrill yelp and dropped a saucepan. They all made for the door except one attendant who rejoiced in the name of Joshua Hazelburnest.

"I must fetch something from my room," he said.

"I won't promise to come to your funeral," I replied.

"It might be difficult to collect all the pieces for a proper burial."

One of the shapelier female servants gave a moan and tottered through the doorway clinging tightly to one of the men, who didn't seem to mind at all. Joshua Hazelburnest looked greenish and came with us. We went by Professor Redlynch's house, which was adjacent to the grounds of the school – too adjacent for comfort. Joshua Hazelburnest and I went in.

"You'd better come along," I advised. "Just in case."

"I couldn't possibly," he began, when, nodding to Joshua, I seized one elbow and he the other. We marched him away, impotently protesting.

I went straight to the Brigadier.

"There may be trouble," I said. "I've done my best, and I hope I've succeeded."

"Quite all right, sir. We'll draw up the tanks."

"I hope they'll be safe."

"The children?"

"No. The tanks."

He looked at me with astonishment.

"Surely not *tanks*?"

"I wouldn't be too sure."

We waited three days. I turned Professor Redlynch over to the police to prevent him returning to his house.

"But – but – my research!"

"How much research does a corpse do?" I retorted, and left him at the police station.

At the end of the three days, we held a conference: the Brig, the Vicar, myself.

"They'll be starving!" was the Vicar's first contribution.

"I hope they will have starved. Then we shouldn't have any trouble."

36

"It's – it's immoral!"

"Is it immoral to hang a murderer?" I was on safe ground here. There had been some particularly nasty murders of young girls a year or so before, and the Vicar had publicly announced his revised views on hanging.

"But the murderer was already dead three days ago!"

"I am trying to protect humanity."

"Is humanity all that important?"

"I am most surprised at your views, sir," I answered. "I should have thought that you, of all people, would have the welfare of humanity at heart."

"I have. But I also believe in the value of souls, even if they be of a different shape from ours. Morality I hold to be universal in the literal sense of the word."

"Believe me, Vicar, these children are wholly evil. They are cruel. They are ruthless. They have no compassion. They have no sympathy. They have no love. You know how Fordson died. And Grahame. Do you want your parishioners, for whom you are responsible, to die in the same way?"

"Gentlemen," interrupted the Brigadier. "Fascinating as this discussion is, we must decide what to do." He looked at me.

"I am willing to go back," I said. "Nothing has happened for three days."

"You expected an outbreak of some kind?"

"If the children were alive, I should have expected all hell to have broken out. Sorry, Vicar."

He smiled a thin smile. "Unlike many of my colleagues, I believe in hell. I'll come with you."

I was startled, but he shook his head at me.

"It is my duty, and I shall do it. Besides," he added wryly, "I am supposed by many to be an expert in good and evil."

The three of us went, flanked by soldiers and escorted overhead by a totally useless helicopter.

The place was absolutely quiet. Every exit was covered by soldiers, and one abruptly kicked open the schoolroom door. I went in first, the Vicar following.

They were dead, lying where they had fallen. Some of the tables and chairs had been smashed. Two of my dictionaries were in shreds. There was a hole in the interior wall, displaying a part of the contents of a store-cupboard.

The blackboard had been turned round, and there was my last message in it. The Brig read it with sardonically raised eyebrows. "So that's how you did it!"

I nodded. Somehow, I felt no satisfaction. The term was over, but I was beginning to miss my most brilliant class of students.

The vicar was gently examining the bodies.

"Different," he murmured. "Their faces seem – peaceful."

I glanced at Olaf and Freya. It was evidently Olaf who had made that hole in the wall, but there was no sign of violence on his face. Or on the face of Anna, who was lying amid the ruins of two tables.

"Are they all here?" enquired the Brig sharply. "I thought there were six."

"One's upstairs," I replied. "He died before – before all this." I gestured to the litter of wood and paper, and the debris of plaster from the wall.

"But six?" insisted the Brig.

I looked quickly around. Olaf, Freya, Anna. "Jack was complaining of a headache. I sent him to lie down."

The inner door opened. A soldier entered. "There's one at the bottom of the stairs. He looks as if he's fallen down. Brown hair and eyes. He doesn't appear to have hurt himself, but he's dead."

They were all lying with their eyes open and blank.

"That will be Jack. Frank's probably on his bed. Have a look, will you?"

"Yes, sir." The soldier withdrew.

"There's one more," I said.

"Behind the blackboard." The Vicar had spotted her.

I went and pulled the blackboard out from the wall. Yes, it was Barbara. With her dark eyes open, but indisputably dead, she held a piece of chalk in her hand. Why? Then I looked at the back of the blackboard. Written in Barbara's characteristic handwriting, angular, passionate, but clear and legible.

"My teacher. My darling teacher. I love you. I tried so hard to learn. For you. I love you. I love you. I love you. I love y—" The rest of the word was a diagonal scrawl of chalk.

I stood there, bending over the dead body, her brown eyes looking up but not seeing me. Not seeing anything.

"She *is* dead?" It was the Brigadier's voice.

"Yes. She's dead." I tried to make my voice non-committal.

"Then we'd better clear them away."

"Carefully," interjected the Vicar.

"Yes, sir. We'll be very careful."

They fetched Frank's body down from his room and brought Jack's in from the foot of the stairs where he had fallen. Soldiers were set to dig a communal grave in the corner of the school grounds. They carried the bodies there on stretchers. The Vicar went with the first. I don't know if he said any kind of prayer as they were laid side by side in the hole. They came for Barbara last. I had taken my handkerchief, licked it, and rubbed out Barbara's message. Those last words were for her and me alone.

"Not this one," I said quickly. "I'll take her." The body was surprisingly light.

I bought a plot in the municipal cemetery, and laid Barbara's body in it. A simple headstone gave her name, Barbara, and the date we had found her body. That was all.

The Vicar had a stone on the other grave, with five names on it. Under, he had added a text that I didn't recognise: "Other sheep have I".

I planted flowers on Barbara's grave. I go there every Sunday. I'm not a religious person, so I don't know what to say. But I kneel on a bit of plastic to keep the damp from my knees. And I say: "God, if there is a God, teach me what to do next time, if this happens again." Then I stand up, collect my piece of plastic, look at the headstone, and say to myself, "Barbara, my darling Barbara, I love you."

And like a weak, silly, sentimental fool, completely unsuited to be in charge of anybody or anything, I come away. I've seen other people looking at me strangely, but I don't care. I don't care. I don't care. And I'll come next Sunday, and the Sunday after that, and the Sunday after that, while I have my health, and even if I haven't, I'll crawl here on my hands and knees. And they'll bury me here – I've put it in my will – in the same grave as Barbara.


**Donald Stevens**

Dr. Stevens is archivist of Christchurch Priory. He has written many short stories and articles, the latter mainly concerned with his work. He is a Fellow of the institute of Linguists, and has frequently visited south-eastern Europe, where many of his short stories are set.

# Touch of Time

"Gabriella, are you coming?" Addison asks. I gulp and nod my head. "Well, come on then." She points to the graveyard across the street. It's so dark I can hardly see what's in front of me. I hear rough breathing and I know Brayden is waiting for me on the other side. I gulp again and force my feet forward no matter how much I want to turn and run. I have to do this. This is my initiation for the Cool Crew.

My eyes are adjusting and I can make out tombstones, crumbled with age. I keep my hand on my flashlight. The metal tube, warming in my grasp.

"All right, get to work." Addison says. Clare grunts and tosses me a can of red spray paint. I catch it with one hand and walk along the rows of grave markers.

**Sarah Johnson 1734-1802**
**Elizabeth Walker 1806-1836**
**Abigail Harris 1799-1826**
**Thomas Lipscomb 1826-1841**

I stop at the last grave, Thomas's. He was just a boy when he died. Only fifteen, like me. I don't have time to feel sorry for him. I squat down and uncap the paint.

"Hurry up, Gabriella!" Brayden whispers. "I can see headlights." I turn and look. Two white lights stand out in the dark. They're travelling farther down the road, toward us. I press the trigger and a fine line of red mist shoots out and splatters against the tombstone. I've only completed a few letters when the headlights come to a stop at the edge of the cemetery. I switch off my flashlight and hold my breath. I can feel my heart pounding in my ears.

"Let's get out of here!" Clare shouts nervously behind me and takes off into the bushes. I try to finish writing my name but I can't see without my flashlight. I grab the cap off the ground and take off running after the Cool Crew.

"Wait up, guys!" I whisper, but they can't hear me. They've left me behind to get caught.

I'm running without watching my feet and I trip on a rock, jutting from the dirt. I fly, arms sprawling, my head smashes into a tombstone and then everything goes black.

My head is hurting and I feel sleepy.

"Are ya alright there, darlin'?" a boy's voice says. I open my eyes slowly and allow them adjust to the brightness of the sun. "Ya took quite a spill."

A boy in his mid teens stands over me. His dark black hair flops over his green eyes. I'm scared of getting in trouble so I jump up and start to run, but he catches me easily and holds me to his body so I can't escape.

"Don't be afraid. I ain't gonna hurt ya," he says.

"They made me do it! I'm sorry," I cry. He loosens his grip and looks deep into my eyes. I squirm in his grasp.

"What're ya talkin' bout?"

"The Cool Crew. It was all part of their stupid initiation and I shouldn't have done it. I'm sorry." He looks at me with his eyebrows scrunched up, like he can't understand me.

"I don't know what ya talkin' about, we're the only ones here." I look around and see that he's right. Only, I don't know where we are.

"Where's the graveyard?"

"You mean the church? It ain't much of a graveyard, only got a few people in it." He drops his eyes, seeing something I couldn't.

"Only a few? But there were hundreds," I say, still looking around. I want to back away but he's holding my arms too tight.

42

"Nope, it's the only one we got 'round here. You feelin' okay? I can get old Doc…"

"No, I'm fine. I have to find my friends. I bet they're looking for me," I say and he lets go of my arms. I start to walk away from him but he follows me.

"You gotta name?" he asks.

"Gabriella," I say, refusing to make eye contact with him and hoping he'll leave me alone.

"That's a strange name," he muses.

"It is not," I say defensively. I stop walking and turn to look at him. "What's your name, then?"

"You talk funny, girl. Where ya from? You ain't from 'round here, are ya?" he says, ignoring my question.

"Dallas."

"Dallas? I never heard of no Dallas before," he says and scratches his head.

"Don't you go to school?" How can he not know where Dallas is? It's the city next to here.

"I don't go to school no more. I work in the fields," he says with a crooked smile. He looks no older than I am. How can he have a job? He's sixteen at the most. And what field is he talking about? I shake my head.

"Well then mysterious boy, maybe you should go back to school," I say and turn to leave again but he stays at my elbow. I toss my hair over my shoulder and wipe the sweat off my brow.

"Gabriella!" he sounds shocked. He reaches out and grabs my wrists, making me jump.

"What? Let go." I twist in his grip, but he's strong. He's fixated on something on my head. I turn away from him. "Please, let me go."

"No, you need to see old Doc," he says and puts a hand on my forehead. "Your head's bleedin'" I reach up and touch the sore spot over my left eye and pull my hand

43

back. It's covered in blood.

"Here," he says and hands me a white rag from his pocket. I take it cautiously and hold it to my head. He pulls me by the elbow and starts walking. "I'm takin' ya to old Doc. He'll know what to do."

"I'm fine," I say, but he doesn't listen.

We come across an old barn. It's rickety and falling apart. I wonder why it hasn't been torn down yet. It looks like a death trap. I want to ask the boy, but it seems silly so I keep quiet. When we get behind the barn I can see a whole town, only it can't be a town. The buildings are old and worn, smoke pours from chimney's even though it's a warm summer day. People are walking around going from door to door wearing... I strain my eyes. Wearing dresses and trousers and buttoned shirts and suspenders. What *is* this place?

"Doc's place is just up here on the corner. Ain't no better doctor around for miles," the boy says.

"Where are we?" I ask. Fear boils in the pit of my stomach. Something's not right here.

"This is the town. Don't ya know where we at? Must a hit your noggin pretty hard."

"I mean, are we at a re-enactment of some kind?" I scan the crowd, everything looks so real, so old. Like I've taken a step back in time.

"Re-enactment?" He shakes his head and his hair falls into his eyes, he swats it away with his hand and his eyes slide over my face with concern. "Come on, we're almost there."

We walk down a small slope and the boy holds my hand to keep me from falling. Once we're safely at the bottom, he leads me to a building that's separated from the rest. He

44

knocks on the door.

"Doc! Ya in there?" There's a shuffle behind the door and an old man pokes his head out.

"Keep it down, Tom. I've got patients in here tryin' to sleep." The old man looks at me and then I see his eyes trail up to the drying blood on my forehead. "What happened?"

"Don't know. I found her near the graveyard," the boy says. The old man reaches out and I flinch.

"Let's sit her down," he says. They both lead me to a chair on the outside of the building. I sit down and fold my hands in my lap. Doc is an intimidating man. His wiry white hair only has a tinge of rust colour left. His teeth are crooked and yellow and his eyes are gray and bright. He probes my forehead and I wince under his rough, calloused fingers.

"She don't know where she is," the boy says.

"Where did you say you found her, Tom?" The boy's name is Tom? Why is that familiar?

"Near the graveyard," he says and sits down next to me.

The graveyard. The spray paint. The Cool Crew. The grave. Thomas Lipscomb. But it *couldn't* be. That was years ago! I must have hit my head really hard. I closed my eyes and tried to focus.

"Young lady, what is your name?" Doc asks.

"Gabriella."

"Do you know where you are?"

"No, sir."

Doc shakes his head and looks into my eyes. I'm sure he can see my fear deep down, showing through my irises. I want to look away but his gaze holds me to the spot.

"Tom, go and fetch my kit from under the first bed. Be sure to keep quiet."

45

"Yes, sir." Tom gets up and goes into the building and leaves Doc and me alone.

"Don't worry, Gabriella. I'll fix you all up," Doc says. I nod because I'm lost for words.

Tom returns and Doc cleans my wound. He puts gauze over it to keep it clean.

"Ya wanna stay at my house?" Tom asks me after we've left.

"I really need to get home."

"Ya don't know where home is."

I scowl at him and realize he's right. I have no idea where I am anymore.

"Well, it's almost time for supper and I'm starvin' and momma won't like me gettin' home late," he says and pulls my arm. "She always makes extra in case someone stops by. Come on."

"Fine."

"First we gotta get you cleaned up. I don't know why ya wearin' your underclothes in front a people."

"Underclothes?" I look down at my blue jean shorts and plain black tank top.

"And strange ones at that," he says with a laugh.

"These aren't underclothes."

"Well, they ain't a dress." He arches one eyebrow and it wrinkles his forehead.

"Girls don't always wear dresses where I'm from," I say and toss my hair back over my shoulder. It's really getting hot out here. I squint and look up at the sun. Not a cloud in sight.

"What do they wear then?"

I gesture down to my body. "This. Sometimes pants, when it's cold."

"Girls wear pants?" His jaw drops open and then he snaps it shut.

46

"Yeah, so what?"

"You're a strange girl, Gabriella. It's like you're from another time. But I think I like that." He smiled a crooked smile that made his eyes squint. I feel my cheeks redden and burn so I look down.

"Well you're the one from another time. It's like you're stuck in the past."

"If I'm stuck in the past, does that make ya from the future?"

"I guess so," I say and smile. Then a thought hits me. "Are you Amish?"

"What's that?"

"You know like, you don't use electricity or cars or anything."

"I don't know what ya talkin' about." Tom stops suddenly and points to a small house surrounded by trees and bushes. It looks like a log cabin. "That's my place."

"It's pretty." It looks like something from a postcard. Trees linger around the edge of the property and flowers are scattered throughout the yard.

Tom takes me inside and gives me his sister's dress for me to wear. I change into it and brush through my hair with my fingers. This dress is plain and simple, but beautiful at the same time.

"Ya look nice," Tom says as I exit the room.

"Thanks."

"Is that my dress?" a girl behind him asks.

"Yes, Jane," he says.

"She isn't keeping it." She didn't say it hatefully, but it made me flinch.

"I'm sorry, he said I could borrow it," I say timidly.

"That's fine. It's not everyday he brings a girl home to meet the family. I'm Jane, his older sister."

"Hello." I smile sweetly and Tom takes my hand.

47

"Where's everyone else?"

"Already at the table," she says.

Tom leads me to the kitchen and introduces me to the rest of the family. His mother welcomes me with open arms and starts spooning food onto my plate.

"We don't have much food, but we share what the good Lord gives us," she says with a warm smile. I look over at Tom who's suppressing a grin.

"May the Republic of Texas live on," his father says and then holds his cup up. The rest of the family does the same, so I raise mine too. We all clank glasses and take a sip. A memory from 9$^{th}$ grade surfaces in my head. A history lesson. It confuses me.

"Republic of Texas, you mean the United States? We haven't been our own country since 1846," I say. The table goes silent and every eye flickers to me. "Don't you know what year it is?"

"Don't you? It's 1841," Tom says.

I drop my cup and it clatters to the ground, spilling my water all over my dress. I can feel my mouth hanging open but I've forgotten how to shut it. Slowly my brain begins to make sense of it all. Thomas Lipscomb died in 1841 and Tom is sitting next to me.

"What's your last name?" I ask.

"Lipscomb. Thomas Lipscomb."

I open my eyes I'm laying in a bed with a wash cloth over my head. I must have passed out.

"Poor dear, doesn't know what year it is," his mother says over my head. She looks down and pats my shoulder. "There, there, dear. Just relax."

I spend the next few days recovering and trying to find a way home, but I have no luck. Mrs. Lipscomb tells me I can stay with them for as long as I wish. Tom never leaves my side except to go to the fields to work. Those long hours are the hardest. I've grown accustomed to his constant yammering in my ear.

It's a dark and stormy day but I walk to the fields to meet Tom. He looks tired but smiles when he sees me. I run up to him and he hugs me. We walk side by side back to the house. Thunder rumbles over our heads, as we try to hurry back.

A rabbit darts out from the bushes along the path and tries to run across the dirt road in front of us. It's hind leg is hurt and it limps pitifully.

"Let's catch it," Tom says and takes off after the rabbit before I can say a word.

We come across the old brown barn that now leans to its side. Tom starts running toward it.

"Don't go in there, that thing could fall!" I shout at him.

"Don't worry, I'll be fine."

"Tom, please don't." The clouds are so thick, they block out the sun. It's starting to rain and I hug my arms around me.

"I'll be right back. Then we can go back home and mama can cook us up some rabbit stew." He smiles that crooked grin and takes off after the injured creature. He disappears behind the barn door and I can't see him anymore.

I wait on the balls of my feet. The wind has picked up and a flash of lightning lights the sky with an eerie glow.

"Tom, leave it. We have to go," I yell over the howling wind. I can feel my heart beating faster. Something's not right. I don't like the way the barn sways in the wind. A loud wailing noise rips through the sky and I jerk my head around to my left and see a funnel of wind come down and kiss the ground. "TOM!"

The barn shakes and groans. I don't think. I take off running and I'm in the barns doorway in a flash. "Tom!"

"I've almost got 'em." Tom's concentrating on the rabbit's hiding place.

"Tom, we've got to take cover. There's a tornado coming." Tom looks up at me and his eyes get big. I turn and see the twister heading straight toward us. He grabs my arm and we burrow deeper inside the barn. We quickly stack bails of hay and create an igloo for protection but I know it's no use. I poke my head out and watch the storm come closer. I've never been more scared in my life. I can feel my body trembling, but can't bring myself to stop.

Cattle are running loose now and mooing frantically, seeking shelter. The fence must be busted. I see one cow split from the herd and head straight for our hiding spot. I look over at Tom who's pulled his knees up to his chest. He looks scared, but I know he doesn't mean to show it. He doesn't see the cow. It's coming closer. Too close.

"Tom!" I throw my arms out and shove him out of the way at the last second. I can feel the hooves slam into my chest and stomach and then I can't breathe. I'm dying. I can't feel anything but the pain. I want to cry out but no breath leaves my lips. A darkness is tugging at the corner of my eyes. I want to turn and look at it, but my body won't move.

"Gabriella!" Tom shouts over the noise of the storm. I lay there staring at the barn's ceiling. He leans down and pulls my face into his hands. For a second I think he's going to cry, but then he leans down and kisses me. His lips are soft and warm on my cheek and I feel his tears mix with mine. He looks into my eyes.

"Gabriella, that should a been me. Why? Why would ya do that?" His tears are spilling over his lashes and he's

50

choking for air. All I can think about is how green his eyes are. How his face isn't quite that of a man's or a boy's, but somewhere in between. I just want to sleep, I'm exhausted. The darkness is growing, demanding my attention. I close my eyes and fall under its hypnotic spell. The blackness erases the pain and I'm grateful.

"Gabriella, are you okay?" I open my eyes slowly and take one cautious breath. It's still dark outside. Braydon is shaking my shoulder.

"Where am I?" I ask.

"The graveyard. Remember?" I can make out his face hovering over mine. "How do you feel?"

"What just happened?" I sat up and rubbed my head and found a small bump.

"You tripped," Brayden says. "I thought you were behind us, but then when I noticed you weren't, I came back for you. You scared the you know what out of me." He helps me to my feet and I notice the can of spray paint lying in the dirt. I bend down and pick it up.

"I shouldn't have done it," I say. "I shouldn't have come here tonight."

"Hold still." Braydon trails his fingers over my sore head. His eyes widen when he feels the lump. "We need to get you to a doctor."

"That's what Tom said." I throw my head back and laugh. Brayden frowns and holds my shoulders still.

"Who's Tom?" He looks around for something, but I don't know what.

"Thomas Lipscomb," I say. I pull out of his grip. "His grave, I spray painted it."

"I think you're confused, Gabriella." Braydon looks scared. Is he scared of me? I look around, we're the only ones here.

51

"No. His grave is right there." I point to a grave and walk over to it.

"There's no Thomas here," he says.

"Yes, the one I painted." I lean down and smear the wet paint. A name becomes visible, but it's not Thomas Lipscomb.

It's Abigail Harris.

"But his was next to this one!" I search the area but I can't find his grave.

"There wasn't a Thomas here," he says. I think you hit your head too hard. Let's go get you checked out." He pulls my arms and I struggle to get free. He can see that I'm not going to come quietly so he pulls me over his shoulder and starts to carry me out of the cemetery.

We pass the last row of graves and I catch a name on a tombstone.

"Wait! Put me down!" Braydon sighs and then obeys. He sets me down and I walk over to the grave. I squat down and run my fingers over the letters.

Loving husband and father, Thomas Lipscomb 1826-1874

Gabriella 1841

I stare down at the words trying to make sense of them. My name is right there on that tombstone. That can't be a coincidence, can it? Braydon sits next to me and I tell him everything. About Tom. About the barn. About my... death. He holds my head and nods, but I can tell he doesn't believe me.

He pulls me up to my feet and leads me away from the graves and back to the car across the street even though I'm still babbling. He helps me into the car where the others wait.

"Where were you?" Clare asks. She doesn't look worried. I glance over at Braydon who was now sitting behind the wheel. He shakes his head and I know he wants me to keep quiet.

"I fell," I say. "I hit my head and blacked out."

"Oh, well. Glad your fine now," Natalie says. "Welcome to the Cool Crew." She smiles at me and I force myself to smile back. I turn my head to watch out the window and I see the cemetery disappear from view.

**A.J. Spindle**

A. J. Spindle found her passion for writing at the age of seven. She used to write about aliens and talking dogs. Now she writes more exciting stories of love, fantasy, and the occasional non-human. Instead of studying for finals, you can find Amanda slumped over her writing desk, hammering out her new masterpiece. Please visit www.ajspindle.com for more information.

# Earthrights

"Now, tell me, exactly why are you selling the rights to Earth?" said the Chossey.

Bohnan sighed.

He'd already explained the reason in great detail but the Chossey didn't seem to be the brightest spark in the inferno. And to be honest, it was just as well. This deal was important and he didn't want a potential buyer to work out the drawbacks before he signed.

He'd schemed for months and it wouldn't do to lose patience now.

Bohnan the Carbairian smiled winningly with both mouths, gritted his fangs and started again.

"I'm getting old. I want to retire. I have a little holiday home in the Drosophila Galaxy and I'd like to end my days there."

"The *what* Galaxy?"

"Drosophila."

"Never heard of it"

"It's not very well known at the moment but it's a very up-and-coming place. Property prices are set to rocket. If you're interested, I know of a very desirable little place not far from mine."

"Really?" said the Chossey, his single eye lighting up with excitement. "Yes, I would be interested."

"But I digress," said Bohnan quickly, "there's plenty of time to discuss holiday homes after we've settled the ownership of the Earth," he smiled encouragingly with both mouths.

*Steady on old chap,* thought Bohnan. *There'll be plenty of time to sell him property in an imaginary galaxy later.* He just needed the Chossey to sign on the dotted line and then... then, he'd head to the furthest reaches of the universe and live out the rest of his days in luxury.

"You don't look old enough to retire," said the Chossey.

Bohnan paused for a second. Had he underestimated the Chossey? Was he attempting to smooth the deal with flattery? Or worse, was he suspicious?

The blank expression on the Chossey's face suggested that neither explanation was the case. He was like a terrestrial dog with a bone, Bohnan finally decided, he simply hadn't quite absorbed Bohnan's reason for selling the rights and was merely trying to make some sense of it all. The act of information processing was painful to watch, decided Bohnan but he reminded himself that the Chossey's stupidity should work to his advantage.

"It's not so much that I'm old," he began, "but I'm feeling old. You know how it is, some days it's a struggle to get out of bed. I'm tired and I long for some rest. And then again, there's my war wound," he said, rubbing his scaly thigh.

The Chossey nodded sympathetically.

Bohnan pressed on, "And that's why I want to sell the rights to the Earth."

"But you don't exactly own the Earth yet, do you?" said the Chossey.

Bohnan had anticipated this – even the Chossey would have noticed that he hadn't yet staged his invasion of the Blue Planet.

"I've lost interest," he said casually, "I prefer the chase to the kill but I've done the necessary preparation and all that now remains is for someone bold and brave, such as yourself, to walk in and take over."

The Chossey licked his blubbery lips in anticipation.

"Mankind is now in such a weakened state that they'll be unable to resist an invasion," continued Bohnan.

"How d'you know they're so weak?"

"Because I weakened them."

"How?"

"That's part of the deal. I explain how the human race has been completely undermined and how you can claim the Earth's riches... and you pay me three million Goron ducats."

If the Chossey had possessed an eyebrow, it would undoubtedly have shot upwards towards his hairline. As it was, the single eye opened so wide, it was in danger of popping out.

"Th-three million?"

Bohnan fought back the laughter. He'd happily settle for one million but the Chossey had to believe that what he was offering was priceless.

"No," said the Chossey "you're asking too much. No planet's worth that, especially one that's overcrowded with revolting human beings *and* is full of disgusting water".

"Without giving too much of my secret away, that's the beauty of it."

"What? Human beings and water?" asked the Chossey.

"Exactly. The wealth on that planet is incalculable. Trust me, I've been watching the humans for countless Earth years."

"I know," said the Chossey smugly, "we've been watching *you* watch *them*."

"Have you?" said Bohnan in mock surprise.

He knew exactly who was observing him at any given moment and had detected the clumsy surveillance of the Chossey. Interestingly, the objects of his examination, the humans, were completely unaware of his presence or the fact that they'd been monitored for years.

His performance of astonishment at being observed

had fooled the Chossey, who was beaming broadly and Bohnan had the overwhelming urge to reach across and slap the stupid, self-satisfied grin from his face. With great restraint, he resisted and instead, scratched at the scaly creases in his neck. Small insects scuttled out of the deep crevices and darted about in panic over the rough, reptilian skin, looking for sanctuary. Bohnan seized one of the creatures between two claws and studied it absentmindedly.

"Mankind is as vulnerable as this..." he said as he exerted a fraction more pressure on the creature's carapace. The crunch was scarcely audible.

With forefinger and thumb, he flicked the remnants of the helpless bug into the air and wiped his hand down the front of his stained vest.

A cruel gleam lit up the Chossey's eye.

"As easy to crush as that, eh?"

"Easier." Bohnan slid the contract across the desk.

The Chossey picked up the pen.

Bohnan held his breath. Surely he wouldn't be foolish enough to sign without reading it? But there was always hope.

"How?"

"How what?"

"How can they be crushed?"

"You simply land on Earth and take over. There'll be no resistance – I can guarantee that. Then you can just help yourself to the resources. The humans really have been weakened to such an extent they'll surrender without a fight."

The Chossey glanced up at the ceiling with a far away look in his eye.

*He's hooked,* thought Bohnan and held his breath again.

"No," said the Chossey suddenly, "no, the price is too high and I need to know more."

"We can come to some sort of arrangement, I'm sure."

*It's time to exert a little pressure*, thought Bohnan and casually moving his hand under the desk, he pressed a small button.

"Yes, I'm sure we can come to a mutually, satisfactory agreement," he said as a sequence of rapid bleeps rang out.

"Excuse me, please," said Bohnan, pressing a button on the console on his desk.

On the far side of the wooden-panelled room, concealed doors slid apart silently, revealing a screen. There was a click, then it blinked and lit up.

"Bohnan, my old friend..." the face that had spoken, broke up into a series of lines and zig-zags but the voice was still audible. "I hear you're selling the rights to Earth. Don't sell before I get there! I'm just leaving the Drosophila Galaxy – I'll be with you soon."

"Harlix! How good to hear your voice ... hello ... Harlix? Harlix?" said Bohnan, "damn, he's gone..."

"Bad signal," commented the Chossey, who had picked up the pen again. "How long before he arrives?"

Bohnan breathed a silent sigh of relief. The Chossey had fallen for it. He really believed that his ancient rival, Harlix, was on his way and was interested in buying Earth.

It hadn't taken Bohnan long to mock up the communication using a clip of an earlier call from Harlix and then a voice simulator to produce the message and it'd certainly been worth the effort.

"Would you accept one million Goron ducats?"

Bohnan chewed his thumb claw thoughtfully and pretended to consider the offer.

"I was hoping for a bit more than that. Perhaps we

ought to wait until Harlix arrives and see what sort of offer he makes."

"Two million. I can't go higher than that."

"Done," said Bohnan quickly, making the Chossey jump. "Sign here."

The Chossey seemed a bit bewildered by the speed at which Bohnan had agreed and he hesitated.

"Here," said Bohnan tapping the contract with his fore-claw, "and here."

The Chossey laboriously signed the paper twice and looked up.

"Now. I want to know how you weakened the humans."

"I'll tell you everything, when I've seen the ducats."

The Chossey withdrew a large bag from his baggy coat and tipped the contents on to the desk.

"That's one million," he said.

Bohnan banged his fist on the desk.

"We agreed two million!"

"You don't expect me to carry around such large sums, do you? D'you think I'm that stupid?"

Bohnan had scanned the Chossey when he'd come aboard the ship and knew that he had two money pouches in his coat. He seized the contract and pretended he was about to tear it up.

"I knew I ought to have waited for Harlix," he said regretfully.

"Wait! I've just remembered. I brought out a little extra cash this morning."

The Chossey reached into the other side of his baggy coat and extracted another large bag. He tipped the contents on to the pile of coins on the desk.

Bohnan laid the contract down and swept the money towards him.

"Now," he said with a self-satisfied smile, "I'll tell you what I've been up to for the last few years. After much research, I've discovered that water, mixed with human fat can be converted to fuel."

The Chossey gasped, "No!"

"Yes, it's true. There's a whole planet of humans just waiting to be converted to fuel."

"How?" asked the Chossey excitedly.

"Here's the formula," said Bohnan, sliding a large, fat, sealed envelope across the desk "but it'll take a while to read, so best save it for later," he said as the Chossey started to slit the envelope.

"Not that the method is complicated," Bohnan added quickly as the Chossey frowned and looked doubtfully at the envelope, "there's just quite a lot to read, that's all."

The Chossey would find out soon enough that the pages were filled with chemical symbols and scientific formulae that had absolutely nothing to do with fat or fuel but let him do that in his own time.

The Chossey placed the envelope in his pocket and patted it.

"So, how d'you get the fat out of the humans?"

"Just squeeze," said Bohnan, "humans crush remarkably easily."

"How do you get rid of the blood and other stuff?"

"There's such a high proportion of fat, compared to the rest of the body that you don't need to take any special measures. Just press a human, allow the resulting 'soup' to settle and skim off the fat. Simple."

The Chossey was impressed.

"Squeeze, settle and skim," said Bohnan.

"But what happens when the humans run out?" asked the Chossey.

"That need never happen, if you manage them correctly."

"Correctly?"

"Yes, you just need to establish fat farms."

"Fat farms?"

Again, Bohnan had the almost uncontrollable urge to slap the vacant look off the Chossey's face and stop the echo. He moved slightly, jogging the desk and the ducats clinked together, reminding him that he would soon be free... and fabulously rich.

He made an effort to relax.

"Yes, fat farms," he said through clenched fangs, "to breed fat humans."

"But you would need so many humans to make it cost effective," said the Chossey.

"Ah!" said Bohnan; "if you'd been observing the humans closely over the last few years, you'd know..." he held his breath, hoping that in fact, the Chossey hadn't been observing Earth.

"Go on..." said the Chossey.

Bohnan breathed a sigh of relief – obviously he hadn't been monitoring them.

"Well, you'd know what sort of shape the human race was in."

He opened a drawer, withdrew a photograph that he'd previously cut from the *Universal Guinness Book of Records* and slid it across the desktop. He'd carefully removed the caption – "Earth's Fattest Man and Woman"

"They're huge!" gasped the Chossey, staring in fascination. "And that's all..." he said, pointing to the distended, sagging flesh.

Bohnan nodded with satisfaction. "Yes, that's fat."

"Are all the humans that size?" The Chossey's eye was large and round.

"No," said Bohnan, "these are just small ones. Mostly humans are bigger."

The Chossey gasped as his mind played with the possibility of all the fuel that he'd be able to make.

"How did you grow them to that size?" he asked, shaking his head in amazement.

"That's the beauty of it. They do it all by themselves."

Bohnan leaned back in his chair, folded his claws across his chest and smiled smugly.

The Chossey shook his head in awe. "Simply ingenious..."

Bohnan allowed himself the luxury of basking in the glory for several seconds, then abruptly, he scooped up the pile of Goron ducats, deposited them in a leather pouch, which he dropped with a jingle of coins into his baggy coat pocket.

He offered the Chossey his claw. "Well, it's not often that you can say that you gave someone the World and really mean it."

"Sold someone the World, you mean."

Bohnan shrugged. "I'd hate to delay you any longer. I expect you're keen to investigate your new investment and start the squeezing. I'm quite keen to get away on holiday myself..."

"Ah yes, you said you'd let me know about that prime piece of property..."

"I'll be in touch," said Bohnan curtly, herding the Chossey towards the door.

The escape plan had been conceived many months ago and by the time the Chossey realised that Bohnan wasn't aboard the decoy vessel travelling to the Tyrraenic Empire, he would be safely speeding past Capella, towards the outer reaches of the Auriga Galaxy. Two million Goron ducats would buy him anonymity and a life of unimaginable luxury. Goron ducats were highly prized by Aurigans, who were renowned for minding their own business – especially when bribed to do so. Anyway, it would take the Chossey a while to discover that humans were not all as large as Bohnan had led him to believe. That is, if he managed to land at all. There'd been several attempts to colonise Earth and they'd all been met with ferocious resistance. Humans might be ugly, smooth-skinned creatures but they were vicious when roused.

Not my problem, thought Bohnan, as he set his course for the Auriga Galaxy, both mouths grinning broadly.

## Dawn Knox

Dawn Knox has only been writing stories for the last few years although her imagination has been populated by the weird and wonderful since she was a child. She's had two short stories published, one in an anthology of horror stories, called *Shrouded By Darkness*, and another in a sci-fi anthology called *Body-Smith 401*, as well as stories and articles in various magazines.

# Edit Facility

The trouble with students today, Hodgkin thought irritably, is that they have no sense of discipline. He scowled as two of the worst in the day's group jostled each other and decided he'd had enough.

He was a gaunt man, dressed in garb of a curator's uniform that had changed little over the years. Only the Cap on his head marked him out as having a background that demanded respect, something he was determined to get from all who passed through his museum's doors.

"This," he gestured to the machine in front of him, "is what we used when performing operations to inhibit pain. It's called the Calvin Neuro Inhibitor, or more commonly CNI. It replaced conventional anaesthetic procedures during 2036 in most Anglo-American hospitals and became the world standard by 2040. Some of you, if you progress that far in your medical career, may see its latest incarnation in a live surgical environment."

He gazed at them in a manner devoid of expectation.

"As its name suggests it works by inhibiting the neural pathways of the brain. Calvin, as I'm sure you all know" he looked at them sternly "is the name of the museum's patron, Sir Wallace Calvin; the Scottish inventor; born 1972 and sadly died 2055. I'm sure you also all know he ranks highly alongside the former luminary in this field; Joseph Lister."

Hodgkin looked at the group in front of him and realized that only half of them showed a flicker of recognition at the names that were synonymous with the founders of anaesthetic medicine.

Why? Why could they not grasp that to take medicine

forward they must first understand where it had come from?

He sighed, and wondered whether the day would ever come when any student would visit his beloved museum of their own free will rather than as part of their medical studies. He appreciated that becoming a surgeon wasn't easy but thankfully the Medical Board thought it important to teach the next generation how their forebears struggled. Certainly he doubted whether Lister, or indeed Calvin, would have had to put up with such delinquents.

Time for a demonstration Hodgkin decided with a cruel smile. It wasn't protocol, more a case of bending the rules, but it did ensure an attentive audience.

"To illustrate its function I need a volunteer. You, the boy at the back in the red jacket – come here."

"Yeah, go on Red. Show them how it's done" his friend enthused.

Redman, a twenty year-old youth, pushed his way through his classmates with a self-important swagger.

"Name?"

"Johnny Redman, but everybody calls me Red" he grinned, performing a mock bow and some of the students laughed at his clowning.

Hodgkin consulted his *Tablet*. Yes, the young man before him had signed the standard "in the pursuit of learning" waiver; he could proceed. He smiled. What he was about to do was sure to silence him.

Standing in front of the machine Redman watched with interest as Hodgkin switched it on and set the dials before he addressed the students.

"The machine can be set for any time-duration to match the length of an operation. Early machines were built with operator safety limiters but as the anaesthesiologists became familiar with the equipment and the machines themselves more common these limiters became more of a hindrance and were removed. For today's simple demonstration I will calibrate for six minutes; the lowest setting available."

He picked up a skull cap and crooked his forefinger at his volunteer. Redman, his bohemia temporarily deserting him, dutifully moved forward to stand by Hodgkin.

"The effect of using the CNI is to *pause* the brain, or more correctly edit its input so that the patient feels no pain. However, as you are about to observe it also renders inoperative all cognitive thought, but there is no need for alarm and there is absolutely nothing to worry about." Hodgkin gave Redman his most reassuring smile.

"Oh yes, before I forget, what time do you have?" he asked him.

"Two minutes to three. Why?"

"Just remember it."

Redman nodded and Hodgkin continued his preparations. Redman was definitely the better of the two to pick as his friend, like the rest of the group, was quiet with apprehensive curiosity.

Hodgkin placed the skull-cap on Redman's head ensuring the side flanges correctly covered his temples. Then, after cautioning him not to move, he gave the panel one final check before pressing the red button.

As the seconds passed Redman's face changed from tense to calm; blank even. Thirty seconds later a small bleep erupted from the machine's panel and half of its lights dimmed.

"And that's all there is to it" Hodgkin advised the group; now quiet with apprehension. He removed the

66

skull-cap and addressed the silently waiting Redman.

"Red, hold out your right hand, palm upwards." Hodgkin stuck a pin deep into the end of one of Redman's fingers. The group gasped, but Redman didn't bat an eyelid.

Hodgkin stuck a longer pin all the way through the fleshy part of Redman's hand; between thumb and forefinger, and still he didn't flinch. But as one the group gave a shocked cry.

Hodgkin took out a staple gun from his desk drawer and as the students moaned with revulsion he pressed it against Redman's bare arm.

*Wham!*

The students shouted, one girl screamed.

Hodgkin placed the staple gun against Redman's forehead. He paused.

The girl who'd screamed before screamed again, and another joined her. Many students began to look ill and as Hodgkin's finger tightened on the trigger one started to wretch.

Redman stood calmly, a placid look on his face.

*Wham!*

Hodgkin's wrist jerked back with the force of the recoil as the gun shot the metal staple four millimetres into Redman's forehead. Redman remained immobile, his face registering nothing but quiet contemplation.

Hodgkin turned back to the group knowing he had a very attentive audience. "As you can see the subject is totally impervious to pain and provided the implements are removed and the wounds healed before he wakes up he will not even experience a headache." Hodgkin smiled maliciously, savouring the moment.

The group was silent.

"Any questions?"

Nothing. Then as the shock of his flamboyant demonstration wore off a lone hand was raised.

"Wasn't there a military application to the CNI considered?"

"Initially yes, they thought it a wonderful opportunity to insulate their soldiers against the pain of conflict. But, as I'm about to demonstrate, they soon experienced a drawback in that line of thinking."

"Red, follow me, keep up" he instructed and set off with a brisk walk around the room. Redman obediently followed, totally unconcerned about the various pieces of metal protruding from his hand, arm and face.

The room was large, the CNI and students gathered in the centre while the walls were adorned with medical memorabilia leaving more than enough floor space for Hodgkin's purposes. It wasn't the first time he had given such a dramatic demonstration.

Hodgkin quickened his pace, Redman following close behind. The pace quickened again, and again, until the two men were running around the room at full sprint. Then on the sixth lap Hodgkin slowed, and with Redman alongside, returned to where he had started.

"As you can see" gasped Hodgkin, "the subject will blindly follow orders, and it's been determined that if instructed he would have kept on running around the room until he dropped for there is absolutely no intelligence at work."

He bent while he caught his breath, he was getting too old for this sort of thing. A minute later he continued with his narrative.

"Blind obedience may be what's required of a soldier, but equally a people expects its Army to have more sense than that of the common goldfish. Retentive memory is non-operational, and even if something could be taught in this state it doesn't stick."

Hodgkin turned to his charge.

"Red, what is the answer to the sum; two plus two?"

Redman's expression remained blank.

"Two plus two is four, Red. Four. Understand?"

Redman nodded.

"Red, what is the answer to the sum; two plus two?"

Redman remained solidly blank.

"He's got the intelligence of a lump of wood, which I presume is less than his normal self" Hodgkin quipped and his audience hesitantly laughed as he started to remove the pins and staples with forceful tugs. When the CNI gave a shrill bleep, advising him that there was one minute to go before the end of the inhibitor cycle, Hodgkin produced an object which he waved over Redman's wounds.

With ten seconds to go he was finished, all sign of his *attack* eradicated and the dermatology regenerator was once again back in his pocket.

"Three, two, one... how are you feeling Mr. Redman?"

"Fine, get on with it before I change my mind about being your stooge" Redman whined only to look affronted when the rest of the group laughed.

Hodgkin smiled smugly, "I think you'd better check your timepiece. The demonstration was a complete success." Then, ignoring the look of surprise on Redman's face, he switched off the CNI and started for the door.

"Moving on, this way ladies and gentlemen if you please. Through here we have a standard operating theatre of the late twentieth century. Note please, the rudimentary attempts at maintaining a sterile environment..."

His voice faded as he walked and soon all but two of the group had passed through to the next room.

"Hey Red, what was it like? How did it feel? I bet it was great eh?" Jimmy bombarded his friend with questions as he joined him at the CNI's console.

"It was wonderful" Redman lied, unable to admit to his friend he remembered nothing. No memory, no dreams, it was as though he had ceased to exist for every second of the six minutes he had been under the machine's influence.

"I wish it had been me. You get all the breaks, all the fun" Jimmy moaned as Redman inquisitively examined the CNI's controls. Tentatively he pressed a button and the machine sprang back to life.

"Wow."

"Easy" Redman replied smugly, his swagger returning as his embarrassment faded.

"Give us a go."

"Don't be daft!"

"Please" Jimmy implored, wanting desperately to undergo the same experience as his friend. But Redman seemed not to hear as he reviewed the console's dials and buttons. With an exclamation of delight he found what he was looking for.

"You did it! Go one Red, I want a turn" Jimmy pestered until finally Redman turned to his friend.

"Hey Jimmy, I only saw him do it once. It's dangerous," then his grin slid back onto place, "but I'm pretty sure I know what he did. After all if an old duffer like Hodgkin's can operate it then I'm sure I can. What do you say, you *really* want a go?"

Jimmy nodded, his faith in his friend blinding him to the danger. Besides, what could go wrong? Six minutes was nothing and Red said it would feel wonderful. "Come on Red, hurry up and set the thing before we're missed."

"Hang on will you. I want to get this right."

"Hurry!" Jimmy crowded his friend.

"Careful" Red cautioned as his arm was jostled. Damn had he caught that dial? No, everything looked like it had when Hodgkin's had used it. The important number was the six, the display clearly read six.

"Okay, we're on. Right, wear this helmet thing" he passed it to his friend, "that's right, over the temples" but as Redman returned his attention to the machine Jimmy grasped his arm in a surprisingly strong grip. There was worry in his eyes.

"No pain Red, don't hurt me. You don't have a healer."

"What *are* you talking about?" Redman looked at Jimmy with a puzzled expression and Jimmy realized his friend had no memory of what Hodgkin had done. How could he? Jimmy grinned sheepishly and released his grip.

"Sorry Red, guess I'm a bit jumpy. You sure you have this thing set right?" he queried one last time.

Redman nodded, "Look it says six; six minutes Jimmy. Then we catch up with the others."

Jimmy nodded, yeah he thought, six minutes. He could take that, and Red by nature was a "fun guy", not a sadist like Hodgkin. Red wouldn't let him down, Red was his friend. Red was the *best*.

"Do it" he instructed and Redman hit the button and Jimmy's fears and worries were no more.


The Executive Transport glided smoothly into its bay without fuss, exactly as it had done thousands of times previously, yet today something was different. Not that Medical Attendant Caan could put his finger on it.

For weeks now, he realised, Old Red had been on

71

edge. Always an impatient man, determined and possessed of a drive that had diminished little over the years, he had become agitated of late. Maybe it was the passage of years, Caan mused, for Old Red was past the hundred mark and required around the clock supervision. Yet he could see by the display on his wrist that Old Red's biometric implants reported no issues so perhaps what ailed him wasn't medical. Perhaps it was psychological, for Caan with surprise, had finally recognised the emotion his charge was trying so hard to suppress – Old Red was afraid.

"I see Chambers isn't in, as usual" the Old Red snapped in disgust. "The man only ever did know one seven o'clock in the day."

"Sir" Caan dutifully replied as he assisted his charge from the car, surprised that he didn't receive the usual rebuke. Another sign that today was not *normal*.

"Sir, your Cap" Caan held out the small, yet symbolically significant, piece of fabric expectantly. He had nearly missed it, never having known it removed. But Old Red had sat with his head bowed for most of the journey and his Cap had slipped to rest between his feet and rather disturbingly he had not picked it up.

The Cap still remained the badge of accomplishment that all in the medical world aspired. It was more than a badge of identity, it marked you out as a professional. As someone who demanded respect with the greater number of braid *pips* the more respect due. Old Red had more *pips* than anyone else alive, probably more than any other in history. Old Red wore his Cap with pride.

"No, not today" Old Red waved his *badge* aside, much to Caan's astonishment.

"Sir?" Caan spluttered despite a warning glare. He knew how much the Cap meant to his charge; it was incomprehensible he would enter any medical facility without it on his head.

"I said no!" Old Red battered it away, watched with hot eyes as it flew from Caan's surprised grasp to land on the ground. "And stay here, I go in alone" he snapped before awkwardly turning and with the aid of his sticks to lurch towards the door marked 'Staff Only'.

"Not today, not today" he muttered to himself in anger, uncaring that Caan could hear him. "Today I don't deserve to wear it."

Old Red had spent his whole career, his whole life, helping others. He had never married and undertaken more duties and shifts than any other in the profession. He had quite literally lived and breathed the ethos that Medical Staff were there to help. And as he had risen through the ranks he had cut away red tape, interdepartmental fighting and instilled a tremendously high level of discipline – all in the pursuit of better practice. In many eyes he was a hero, always pushing, wanting more from his staff and equipment; desperate to maximise patient care. A desire that hadn't stopped when he had retired, for he had installed himself on the Board of Governors – hounding them to do the right thing, to do better.

More than a little worried Caan picked up Old Red's Cap, carefully blowing away the specks of dirt, then as soon as his charge was out of earshot he activated his communicator.

"Stegen, this is Caan. Yes I know it's early but we have a problem." Caan paused, it wasn't a problem, not really; more of a puzzle. Old Red was perfectly entitled to access any part of the vast complex he chose to, nowhere was barred. But if he did so under his own steam, even aided by sticks and implants, he was going to exhaust

73

himself and it was Caan's duty to make sure Old Red stayed as healthy as possible. It was his only duty, and he intended to perform it to the best of his abilities, regardless of Old Red's mood.

"I need to talk to a nurse, a good one, capable of thinking on her feet. No, I don't think today's visit will be routine."

Nurse Hawthorne watched carefully as Old Red entered her sector. Tired but still upright he was walking with stubborn determination.

*Just be firm, polite and don't take no for an answer*, Nurse Hawthorne reiterated, watching Old Red's progress out of the corner of her eye. Pleased in a way that she was the one selected, but terrified in another.

The sign above the corridor entrance said *Restricted Zone – quiet!* Old Red had personally supervised its fitting. It was the first thing he had done when he took charge of the hospital fifty years previously. Restricted because it was home to patients who required a degree of solitude not available elsewhere, and whose guardians paid handsomely for the privilege. The Solitude Wing was a unique section of the Facility in that there was little in the way of equipment and machinery. No hum of hover-gurneys, equipment with multiple audio readouts or media stations. Even implants, with their barely susceptible motor-whirrs were frowned upon. Which meant Old Red, with his noisy sticks should not be entering; not that he expected anyone to have the backbone to challenge him. Certainly not the young nurse trying to look busy as he made his slow progress down the corridor that would in time lead him to the private room and the Facilities' oldest patient.

Today must be the day, he thought. It had to be! He'd

74

waited so long and this time he must be right about the date. He had an hour in which to get there, plenty of time. Plenty of time for an old fool.

But it seemed he was wrong about something that day.

"I've brought you a wheelchair, Sir" Nurse Hawthorne smiled sweetly as she came abreast of him before executing a neat stop-and-turn so that she was blocking his path. He glared at the most basic and ridiculously primitive of *assists*, as if it was an affront to his sensibilities. Anywhere else the wheelchair would have been cast onto a scrap heap, or into one of the many museums he loathed, but within the Solitude Wing it ranked higher than its more modern counterparts.

"Take that damn thing away" he snarled, "I'm not a ruddy cripple."

"No you're not, but you *are* blocking the corridor" Nurse Hawthorne replied and this time he could detect the steel in her voice. She seemed quite determined, and he smiled to himself. Now here was a girl after his own heart, strong willed and not afraid to improve the lives of those around her, even if one of them was an angry old man with a heavy heart. Not that it meant he would make it easy for her.

"There's no rule that say's I can't make my own way *and* under my own steam" he replied as testily as he could manage.

"Yes there is" she replied with conviction, "rule #692A. Any person or persons moving at less than one kilometre per hour shall be assisted in the interests of efficiency."

He looked at her suspiciously. "Never heard of it."

"Well, it exists, and if you don't accept my wheels then I'm going to turf you out" she seemed quite resolute.

"You know who I am?" he asked somewhat hesitantly,

she had actually sounded like she meant it.

"I do."

Old Red looked at her with keen eyes. Manners, confidence and a determination to see he was cared for. He suspected Caan's hand in the desire but the professionalism was all her own. He was also pleased to note she wore her cap with pride *and* at the correct angle. Far too many were lax in that respect, presenting the mark of distinction at a jaunty angle that mocked their achievement.

He sighed. "All right Nurse Hawthorne, I'll sit in your infernal chair." He grudgingly accepted her assistance and allowed her to stow his sticks on the carry shelf.

"But I want to see that rule at the first opportunity, or you'll be changing bedpans for a week."

"Just as soon as I've written it, Sir" came back her reply and, despite his anger, he gave a bark of laughter.

"I wish there were a few more like you on the Board then I could really retire instead of making all the decisions for the spineless fools on the top floor."

"Sir," she responded concentrating on her manoeuvring.

"You know where you're going? Where I want to be?"

"Yes Sir, to see Mister Wilson. Though I don't know why."

It had not gone unnoticed by the staff that Old Red paid Mister Wilson more than the occasional visit. Nurse Hawthorne had seen him herself but, until ordered, had never dared approach. Like almost all the Facility's staff she was in awe of Old Red. "He is, or rather was, my best friend, many years ago" her charge said and his voice took on a hint of melancholy.

Nurse Hawthorne kept on pushing, attentive and interested.

"There was an accident and I lost him. Killed him

really" Old Red revealed. Then, as though the floodgates opened, he let it all out. He didn't rant or rave, nor did he try and justify his actions; just told it as it was. Told her so someone else would know, and in knowing maybe forgive; for he knew he would never be able to forgive himself.

"Like a child I blamed everyone for my mistake; the undisciplined fool of a curator, the machine's designers, everyone! While all the time I knew where the real fault lay."

Old Red sobbed, "I took my friend's life away and I can never, never, make amends for it. All that I have built, all that I have achieved counts for nothing," he wailed before his voice dropped to an agonised whisper, "I failed my friend and I will take my torment to the grave."

They arrived at the room and Nurse Hawthorne pushed him next to the contented-looking old man in a chair staring out of the window at the sunny day. With a tear in her eye she busied herself with the curtains and turning down the lights. She placed their control in Old Red's hand and gave him a small sad smile. Then, after ensuring he had everything he wanted she exited and gently closed the door.

She looked in from time to time, but saw little change, until almost an hour after she'd left him she heard a low pitched "pinging".

It was Old Red's timepiece and she paused outside the door.

A few minutes later she heard an unfamiliar voice croak, "Wow, it's dark How did it get dark?" Nurse Hawthorne heard his voice take on a worried tone. "Where am I? Red? Is that you Red? You look very old... Yow!

I'm stiff!"

"Jimmy... I'm so sorry..." Redman's anguished voice tailed away and he fell silent.

Jimmy looked down at the paper-thin skin on his hands and flexed his arthritic fingers. Then, as the reality of what had happened hit him, his scream of horror echoed down the corridor.

**Philip T Brewster**

Philip T Brewster loves to write.

Primarily short stories as they fit easier into his busy lifestyle but occasionally, when he finds the time, other projects. His work has been published in several anthologies.

Philip hates waste, enjoys photography and riding his motor-bike which is very practical as he lives and works in and around the city of Leeds, West Yorkshire.

His website is <u>www.philiptbrewster.co.uk</u>.

# Who Will Do It?

Michael watched as Lynn's fists started to clench. Her voice was as sharp as an icicle. "And you, you of all people, have a problem with *immoral*, because?"

Because hacking was unethical, he could have said, even when you hacked into existing records. What she was doing, though, was worse. Far worse. Crossing the boundaries of time. Aloud he said, "Because you're messing with the future!"

"With *the* future, Michael? *The* future? How do you know how many futures there are? Perhaps I'm just changing our own fate, making our future a better place and leaving other futures intact?" Lynn tossed her auburn hair, slowly, elaborately, the way Michael liked, and his body burned for her.

He averted his gaze, fighting the impulse to bend down to kiss her. "And why would you want to do that?"

"Look at the crime rate! Look at our Western society!" Her every sentence was an exclamation, even the rhetorical questions. "Why else would we be living in Thailand? In Thailand of all places? With an alphabet that resembles an orgy of drunken worms? Where only subtle inflections of the voice indicate whether you're asking somebody to pass the salt or to sleep with you?"

Michael let him mind wander. He knew the answers. Thailand was where it was safe to keep the front door wide open, to leave a handbag in one corner of the market while you're haggling in another, where it was safe to walk alone at night. Not that he owned a handbag or wanted to walk anywhere.

"Lynn, we've been through all that. And we've made the decision to move here. So what's the problem?"

"No problem. I simply want to prevent crime. Like any other PI. It's my job to help people."

"Do you know how many murders take place in London alone every day? How on earth can you make a difference?"

Lynn pointed at the screen.

"A girl would have been raped next year at your old high school. I've just made a difference to *her*."

Damn, another power failure!

Just a split second's interruption in the supply, and she had to start all over again. Lynn's fingers moved swiftly across the keyboard. Her eyes left the screen and scanned her surroundings.

It was an elegant office. Dark blue silk curtains and sofas, imported chestnut furniture. So unlike typical PI offices, whose tattered, cluttered and macho features appeared in American detective stories.

"Michael?" she called out impatiently. "Michael, what is your cup doing on the table?"

"Minding its own business," he replied from the doorway. "Unlike you."

"Michael, don't."

"Don't what?"

"Don't mock me. You know that I need a tidy place to work."

"Are you saying that your concentration can be shattered by something as trivial as an empty coffee cup?"

"By that, yes, and by these papers." Suppressing a shudder, Lynn pointed at several envelopes, their flaps ripped open unbecomingly, their contents spilling onto the fluffy carpet.

"Some concentration." Not only sarcasm, spite as well. "I wish you'd stop tampering. Leave the future be. We're

80

living right."

Lynn chose to ignore him.

*Why was the login taking so long?*

The text on the screen scrolled rapidly, making Lynn wish for a better interface. Alas, Win2100 was not, as yet, reliable enough for her purposes. Without major bugs in the present, it seemed to hang the moment she hacked into any future database.

She was always amazed at how easy it had been to circumvent the electronic alarm triggers, to guess the passwords, to tap straight into information that did not yet exist. How did it work, this handshake from the future? Did it resemble Ursula le Guin's ansible, a two-way radio over time, not space? And what gave her the idea that the Internet stretched over time as well as over space in the first place – ah, here it was, the login screen. Lynn entered the password.

Lynn?" Michael's voice came to her as though through fog. Her mind was on the task at hand. She had been wrestling with the puzzle for days now. All the information was there, in front of her, billions of little pixels forming the names, the dates, the facts.

A woman will be shot in ten years' time, right here in Bangkok. The suspects: the woman's brother who was bankrupt and wanted more than his share of the dying father's estate, her husband who wanted to be rid of her for the usual conjugal reasons plus the inheritance, and the husband's mistress. The guilty party will never be discovered. Yet it had to be one of them. She almost had it—

"Lynn!"

Now she looked up, annoyed at the interruption.

"Sweetheart, can't you see I'm—" She noticed the suitcases. "Why?" She leapt to her feet and overturned the computer chair. "Michael, Michael..." No words came. Her mind was blank, her lips dry and stiff. She knew Michael was not taking an impromptu holiday.

Outside, she could hear the noisy engines of tuk-tuks. Even though the room was fully air-conditioned, their suffocating fumes blocked her nostrils and mouth, took her air away.

She forced her brain to concentrate on breathing and pumping blood through her heart.

"It's Sandra, isn't it?" she managed at last.

Michael shook his head. Defiantly. Impatiently. "No, it's not. Although I *am* moving in with her, if that's what you wanted to know."

Lynn could feel the nails of her curling fingers bite into the flesh of her palms. Michael was cruel on purpose, she knew.

"You're moving in with her," she tried to keep her voice steady, "yet she's not the reason?"

Michael pressed the balls of his index fingers into his temples. "Lynn," the word came out as a sigh, "I don't love Sandra. And her apartment is appalling. No aircon, no hot water. But she listens, she really listens when I talk. She cares about my work and whether I've had dinner. You – you don't even notice when I'm around."

"Of course I do."

"Do you? Do you, Lynn? You stare at the computer day and night. You live in the future, solving mysteries that will never take place—"

"If they don't take place, it's because I solve them before they happen. Warn the parties concerned." At the back of her mind, she wondered why was she arguing about that.

"Well." Familiar lines corrugated Michael's forehead. "Here is a problem in the present, for a change. One that is happening right here and now. Deal with it."

He slammed the front door.

Lynn hesitated, then returned to her chair. The murdered woman's brother did not have an alibi for the night of the murder. He was asleep in his bed, he claimed, alone. That did not make him a murderer, not necessarily. The adulterous couple vouched for one another, of course, and that did not make them any less suspect. Right. She could find the guilty party neither by motive nor by alibi.

*How about the way in which the murder was committed?*

A single shot, close range. The bullet penetrated the left chamber of the heart. If it had been strangulation, or another 'typically masculine' method, Lynn would have eliminated the mistress, at least. As it was, all she could do was go through the suspects' data: their credit card transactions, their medical records, the lot.

But she couldn't concentrate. Michael was on his way to Sandra. Soon he would be placing his shirts in her cupboard.

Tears stung her eyes.

*No, hold on, that's not the way. Crying won't solve a damn thing. Think, Lynn, think. What can you do? Come on, you have all the data in the world at your disposal. Data of the future. Go into the records, say ten years on. Does Michael marry Sandra?*

Lynn pulled out the relevant records. *Negative.*

Relief. In two years' time, Sandra marries Mr. Price, the British Consul, and she divorces him just a year later. Price? Price? Sandra Price?

Lynn felt dizzy. Casandra Price. That was the name of the mistress, the suspect in her current case. A coincidence? Price was not an uncommon surname. Search on Casandra Price, previous name Shaw.

Sandra! Did Michael... was he involved? Check the data again, no, no Michael Grant anywhere. Not anywhere? Search for Michael Grant.

The requested record surfaced onto the screen.

CAUSE OF DEATH: ONE.22 BULLET THROUGH THE HEART; DEATH INSTANTANEOUS; BACK ALLEY WEST OF HUALAMPHONG; CULPRIT(S) UNKNOWN.

The date, Lynn could not locate the date. Her fingers were trembling, one of them finally pulled the text further up. The document continued.

INSURANCE POLICY PAID OUT TO MS. SANDRA SHAW ON JANUARY 20TH, 2102.

Next year. What to do, what to do?

Her thoughts were in chaos.

Tell Michael? That's what she usually did – warn the victims, let them deal with it.

This case was different. Would Michael believe her? Strangers usually did when she came to them, an objective outsider, with her fantastic discoveries, "your husband is planning to put arsenic in your coffee, Mrs. Brown".

In this case, though, she was not an outsider, and certainly not objective.

Her heart pounded in her throat.

What's left?

Only one thing.

Bangkok's nightlife enveloped her with the smell of coconut milk, lemon grass and lime. Lynn loved lime, so similar yet so exotically different from lemon. Whenever she smelled lime, she knew she wasn't home, and she loved it.

Tonight, the smell of lime felt alien. She waded

through the small plastic bags on the cobbles, bags that used to hold sugar cane water or pieces of fruit. So much rubbish. Why had she never noticed the litter and the shabby clothes on Milo-skinned people? They worked well into the night, these Asian Tigers, painting silk, sewing, manufacturing more rubbish to be sold to the West and to litter the dumpsters, broken, three days after the purchase date.

Lynn turned into a dark alley, so narrow her extended arms could brush two opposite walls at once. A rat, ginger fur with white socks, shuffled possessively across the alley. She flinched but continued.

How could Sandra possibly live in such squalor? No wonder she wanted a better life. First Michael, then Michael's insurance money, then a husband in the diplomatic corps. And in ten years' time, a lover with a rich wife, with a dead rich wife.

Grimy narrow steps. Lynn listened at the door.

*What if Michael is there?*

*Of course he would be there. Where else?*

*Oh God. How to explain, what to say? Knock on the door, do knock, come on, raise your fist. That's right.*

Sandra's door. So much different from Lynn's solid wood, with her name carved in it. Sandra's door was a limp piece of white board, a map of scratches, a door with its history recorded.

A door that Michael was opening right now.

"Lynn?" His voice sounded gruff. The pale line of his mouth lay perpendicular to the two angry lines above the nose. "What on earth—"

"Read this."

Her hand-held was open on the record describing the tragic demise of Michael Grant. Tab two was Sandra's future marriage certificate. Tab three, Lynn's latest case, the one of the murdered woman with an unfaithful husband.

Lynn didn't wait for him to finish. She turned away from Michael and ran down the stairs, eager to escape the dim corridor, the oppressive smell of rodent droppings, the sight of lotus garlands and the smiling Buddha with his round golden belly.

The fast, heavy beat of Michael's heart had nothing to do with the long climb up the stairs. The solid wooden door, so different from Sandra's, opened without a sound. The room was dark, except for the soft blue glow emitted by the screen. Michael switched on the light.

"Lynn? May I come in?"

"OK. I – I must have dozed off."

His chest felt too small for his heart.

"Will you forgive me?"

She shrugged. "I suppose I have no choice in the matter."

Michael had prepared himself for tears, recriminations as well as the silent treatment He thought he'd covered all options. He'd been wrong.

What now? A bloke could never go wrong with playing dumb. "Huh?" He hoped it was a sexy huh.

"Look at the screen."

He stared at a marriage certificate. His. And Lynn's. The date was three months in the future.

A bubble of contentment radiated to his limbs. "Let's not do anything to jinx it," he said.

Lynn's smile told him she intended to take full advantage. He didn't mind.

It was many, many months in the future now.

So, to summarise." The boss leaned back in his chair.

"You are implying that just because we perceive time as flowing in one direction, it does not necessarily mean that there really is a difference between the past and the future."

"Exactly," the Intelligence MD tried to sound as dispassionate as possible.

*Dispassionate yet authoritative. No emotion. Facts, facts, drown him in facts.* He has to approve the project. "The idea that the past is not constantly influenced by the future is an illusion, a projection of our own temporal asymmetry." *Lots of buzzwords. Good.*

The boss was better. "By the same argument, things we do in the present should change the past."

"From our perspective, the past has already—"

"Happened?" quipped the boss.

"—taken account of what we are doing. If we decide to do something different, the past already knows it. Quantum physics agrees. If signals from the future play a part in determining the outcome of quantum experiments—"

The boss interrupted again. "I'm interested in immediate applications."

"Yes, sir." *Easy now. Easy. Unclench your fists.* The whole future, the whole past, depends on it. "The most rewarding application of this theory would be to make the Internet stretch not only over space, but also over time."

"Why?"

"So we could tap into databases that don't exist any more. Or into databases that still have to be created."

The boss drummed his fingers on the antique desk, extravagantly and wastefully made of pure wood. "Don't we run the risk of people from the past tapping into our database?"

*Cautious bastard.*

"Not a chance, boss," Lynn shook her head. She knew her hair was still attractive, the occasional grey strands emphasizing the richness of the colour. She tossed it back with confidence, aware of the effect it still had on men. "I'll be personally responsible for the security on the time gates. Passwords, electronic security guards, the lot."

**Yvonne Eve Walus**

Yvonne Eve Walus is a novelist. She's been writing for the last two decades because she doesn't know how to stop. Her web page can be found on http://www.yvonnewalus.com on all the past, present and future Internets. Yvonne would like to thank Richard Feynman for all his quantum ideas as well as his awesome book, *Surely You're Joking...*

# The Hollow Statue

**Dear Mr Eden,**
We are sorry to inform you that you have had a number of illegal thoughts this week.

The statue has registered 153 discordant thoughts between 19 February 2034 and 26 February 2034.

You have exceeded this year's acceptable thought life quota and have 0 remaining allowances.

You have already been warned several times. Any further unacceptable thinking will be taken as a direct attack on the Government and will result in appropriate neurological correction. You will also be removed from your post as maths teacher. Remember it is the duty of every citizen to control their own thought life – to secure a peaceful future.

**Yours sincerely,**
**The Department of Peace.**

Richard Eden put the letter down on his desk. He picked up a small bag of birdseed and walked over to a makeshift birdcage where his only pet lived. Inside the cage, a single white dove peered quizzically back at him through the wire mesh. He tried to open the seed packet, but his hands were shaking so much that it ripped open and seed sprayed out across the floor. He dropped to his knees, trying to scoop it up. It was expensive these days and was on the Government's ration list. Above him, his dove began to flap violently against the sides of the cage. That was when he let his head fall and began to sob, letting months of frustration flow out in the tears.

Monday was a dull, depressing morning. The sun looked jaundiced in the sky, as if it were too old. Richard

89

looked out of the train window and then turned back to his neighbour, Thomas. They were travelling in a packed train towards the city for the morning gathering.

No-one on the train was talking. The atmosphere felt as cold as the day. Richard, wondered what it was that made people's hearts grow so cold towards each other. Eventually he broke the silence.

"It's the same each day. It's a different year but the same old stuff. Can't you see that Thomas?"

"For God's sake, keep your voice down," said Thomas eventually. "You sound like some loopy frustrated anarchist... and you know what they do to people like that."

Richard raised his thick eyebrows. "I know they feel threatened by free-thinkers and that the stuff we're hearing is just the same thing told over and over. I've read the old books. They don't let us see what things were like before the revolution because they know it was better back then."

Thomas was listening, but holding his head slightly to the side as if he was being slapped with an invisible hand.

Richard continued, "And they don't like people to ask questions anymore. Questions like why do we have to have a war to get peace?"

Thomas turned around sharply. "The statue tells us we're to forget the ghosts of the old century. 'Leave the old things to die', it warns us. Things are better than they ever were, we're fed and given work. You'd do well to learn from the Government and start to free up your own diseased mind. I'm seriously thinking of breaking our friendship."

Richard ignored the contempt in Thomas's words and replied with what he hoped sounded like a new-found conviction.

"The Government say they care for the people and then tell us we can think what we want... as long as it's what they want us to think. And how free are we to think

90

what we want when we're sitting in front of the statue like… like school children at an assembly?"

The train entered a tunnel for the city centre station. Richard always felt it was as if the city was suddenly swallowing them. They left the train and joined a crowd of people all heading towards the statue. Soon they had reached specially marked places on the paved city centre square. The two men walked among the crowd. People were starting to sit cross-legged, each on their own numbered concrete slabs. Not far away was the statue itself – a massive stone structure with its arms stretched into the air. Sitting in front of the statue every day like this was compulsory. For an hour everybody had to stop what they were doing and gather to listen to the Government broadcasts which came out of the statue's mouth. Anyone who had to work during this time needed a special pass.

"I've asked that you be moved from your place next to me." Thomas pointed to Richard's new space near the front. Richard simply shrugged and walked away. His new place was directly in front of the statue's right foot. It loomed in front of him like an overbearing parent. The statue was eighty metres tall and made out of a rough stone outer shell. It was humanoid, naked but sexless. It was positioned just in front of the new town hall and stood taller than the pillars there. It had been there for over fifteen years – since the revolution.

With the familiar noise of hidden motors, the head of the statue turned, revolving left then right slowly, as if surveying the people below. The eyes, thought Richard, always looked down on them like a disapproving teacher would look down on a class of misbehaving schoolchildren. The Government told the people that the statue could read thoughts simply by looking at them. Richard doubted this was true. It was far more likely, he believed, that work colleagues or neighbours informed the Government about any unconventional personal attitudes. But the fact that everyone believed that the statue could read minds was testament to the influence the Government... and the statues held over the population. There was a statue in every city in the country.

The statues had been heralded as the culmination of the communications revolution. They were the result of a kind of revolution which spread around the world fifteen years before. It had been as if the world had one day decided its thinking had been all wrong in the past and become determined to change. Of course, it was a war which had started all this... but that was history... something which the Government didn't like people to think about. Richard considered the statue to be like the bastard offspring of past technological progress. The statue projected images from its belly button. It projected a holographic image onto clouds above everyone's head. These clouds were artificially formed by gases which sprayed out from the statue's outstretched fingertips every morning. The smell from the gas always reminded Richard of ammonia, but he wasn't a chemistry teacher and nobody asked what was in the gas these days – at least no-one who was still alive. Sound came out of the statue's mouth where the stone lips clamped open and shut noisily. Richard sat almost directly underneath it, close enough to kiss its right foot. He wondered if that would please the authorities.

Soon the cacophony of voices in the square died down. The statue's mouth began to bang open and shut and everybody looked up into the sky. Huge 3D images of world leaders could be seen sitting around a table. The statue's booming voice, monotone and lifeless, echoed around the square:

"**An unprecedented peace deal has been signed**

**today at a meeting of the united world order. This historic deal will promote better trade links between participating countries. Better trade equals a better economy and a better economy equals better living conditions and services. But this peace, real peace, has come only through a harsh fight with non-member states. Only through the continued resistance of these countries can we continue to secure this real peace and the living conditions. In the future we confidently predict that every town will be linked up to the Global Statue Network.**"

Richard wondered how this would happen when many war-torn countries had towns in which there was not even any electricity.

"**The deal ratifies the previous peace deals signed last year and the year before and is a fresh reminder of the commitment of our leaders to combat our common enemies and to secure continued peace.**"

Then the image of the leaders faded and the face of a blonde-haired girl of about ten appeared. She was smiling down at everyone benevolently.

"**Of course,**" continued the statue, "**today's children have not been jaded by exposure to the past. They know nothing of the old systems we grew up with before the revolution. We should think only about a future, where their interests are placed first.**"

Richard got cramp in his neck at this point and had to move his head. The statue continued relentlessly:

"**They are the innocent ones. Their thoughts are faultless. They demand real peace and unity and harmony. It is our duty to live up to these demands and to think accordingly.**"

Richard was massaging his neck when he first noticed the hole. It was hardly bigger than the size of his hand and

93

hidden just behind the giant foot in front of him. He was positioned in such a way that he was the only person there who could see it. He looked away quickly, just avoiding the statue's eyes as the whole head bowed forwards to look at the people at the front. Although he knew the statue couldn't read his thoughts, he began to think about complex equations at that moment.

The rest of the day was spent trying to concentrate on teaching rowdy children how to do basic algebra. Later he was summoned in to see the head teacher of the school.

"I've decided to let you teach the bliss-children this afternoon."

The head-teacher, a waspish looking woman in her fifties, smiled and held up a hand to stop Richard's protests. No-body liked trying to teach the bliss-children. They were kept on the top floor, separate from the others. Richard rarely saw them because there were already five thousand children at the school and only about ten bliss-children. But it was easy to recognise one of them.

"Our hope is that the experience brings you to your senses regarding your unacceptable thought-life."

The head-teacher accompanied him up the stairs to the top floor. He felt genuinely afraid. As they approached the door he felt as if he could barely breathe inside. She opened the classroom door and introduced him to the class. The children sat motionless in their seats, as still as statues. They were aged between ten and thirteen. One of them looked a little like the blonde girl from the earlier broadcast... except part of her head was missing. Her hair had been shaved down one side. Each child had had an operation to correct their thinking. The procedure had left a deep chasm in the side of their heads. Richard could tell which children had had the operation most recently because their thick, white scars were still visible inside the shaved section of hair.

"You should have no trouble keeping them under control," said the head-teacher as she closed the door behind her, leaving Richard with the children.

It was a joke in bad taste. All through the 'lesson' (if that's what you could call it) none of the bliss-children talked or whispered to each other. They looked happy enough, but Richard thought they were also a little like automatons because they never asked questions. They did exactly as they were told. He tried to concentrate on the whiteboard, but halfway through he stopped, turned and asked the question which had been jangling around inside his brain since he had entered the room.

"Why did they operate on your heads?" he asked, looking intently at each face, searching for an answer.

But the only reply came from a boy at the back of the room, whose voice sounded too similar to the monotone drone of the statue.

**"Because of the past. Because we were broken."**

"But, what did you *do*?" Richard couldn't think of much that deserved such punishment.

The boy looked directly back at Richard. **"Our imaginations didn't work properly. They had to be fixed."**

When Richard left that afternoon he felt only despair.

That night he went to bed early and had a feverish nightmare. Images filled his mind of the misshaped heads of the bliss children. They looked back at him with the eyes of the statue. Then he was sitting next to the statue's foot, trying to solve a complex equation written next to the hole. Unless he could solve the equation he knew he was doomed to live a kind of half-life. But it was too hard. And something was moving about in the hole. It was scraping and getting closer but he was too afraid to look. Suddenly he woke to the sound of his dove flapping its wings against the wire mesh.

Richard got up and went across to the dove, taking it out of its cage and holding it to his chest. It felt warm and soft and didn't try to fly away. The things he did next were an act of sheer desperation.

Closing the door to his flat behind him he boarded the late train service and headed towards the city centre. This time the train was almost deserted. He clasped his coat tight around him and stared at the reflections in the window. He wished himself into the dimly lit train window world that was a reflection of his reality and tried to imagine it was a happy, love-filled place. For a brief moment he felt numb and cocooned. But when he entered the tunnel and the city ate the train, the austere reality of his life hit him once again.

The city centre was dark and deserted. The pubs and clubs, along with the shops had long since relocated to the suburbs. The statue stood solitary and motionless, its mouth and eyes closed. The sky was clear and he felt strange being there in the dark without the manufactured clouds. The statue was an eerie black silhouette in the moonlight. He walked past the empty places to the statue's heel and took out the dove from inside his coat. The bird had been fluttering about next to his chest, fluttering like his heart was. Without ceremony Richard pushed the white dove through the hole, pressing his hands against the space so that the dove would fly up into the hollow leg. For a while it flapped against his hands, but soon he heard it moving further up the leg and he was able to move his hands away. He then took out an old T-shirt from his coat pocket which he used to plug the hole. He waited for a while, sitting on a toe. There were no more noises. He supposed that the dove had landed somewhere inside. He hoped that it would somehow cause some damage to the statue and walked back to the train thinking through his hopes. If it did work, if the bird wrecked the statue, then other people would hear about it. People still travelled. They would hear about the statue which broke down and realize that the Government wasn't infallible and unquestionable. People would start thinking for themselves again. Perhaps there would even be a counter-revolution. Not for the first time, Richard found that he hardly dared to think.

The next day it was raining; heavy droplets pelted the train window. Thomas was reading one of the newspapers which the Government owned and edited.

"These are such cleverly written articles," said Thomas, lifting his paper towards Richard's face. "The Government is so considerate of our needs don't you think?"

Richard shrugged. "They certainly seem to have summed up our priorities correctly."

Thomas smiled then and slapped Richard on the back, "Once a maths teacher always a maths teacher, there's hope for you yet, citizen."

The statue's voice came loud and clear:

**"We must break from the past if we hope to forge a brighter future for ourselves and our children. To this end we ask every citizen to hear the plea of our world leaders and of the statues. A further peace deal has been signed. The ratification of today's pafe deal waf frtfer chmphd b..."**

There were gasps from the people. Then, out of the statue's mouth, a tiny white dove's head appeared and looked curiously down at the people below. The bird began to emerge from the mouth, ready to soar into the sky. Richard felt a surge of hope. But then, suddenly, horribly, the statue's mouth clamped hard shut over the dove as it was half out. He stood up, placed his hands over his head and watched as the bloodied front half of the dove fell down the length of the statue and landed in a messy heap on the concrete floor.

"It's been divided into two!" shouted Richard hysterically.

The operation didn't take long. It was considered a success. His position at the school was soon filled by another eager young maths teacher. He spent a lot of time alone in his flat looking at the empty birdcage. In his hand, unopened, he held another letter from the Government. It read:

**Dear Mr Eden,**

**We are pleased to tell you that you have had an entire year free of illegal thoughts.**

**As a reward for being such an outstanding citizen we are sending you a year's free supply of birdseed. We have forgiven you for the past and are pleased that you can now look forward to a peaceful future.**

**Yours sincerely,**
**The Department of Peace.**

**Nick White**

Nick White is a writer living in Staffordshire. His website is www.nickwhitewriting.com. This story is dedicated to his wife, Jen.

# Heavy Air

Roop closed his nose vents and drew breath through his teeth as he peered through the waste ejection flue of the Trade Imperium freighter. The pink-faced Earthers were in such a frowning hurry that they barely noticed the stowaway Vendonaxan as he emerged onto the trade dock's gangways, and those that did carefully stepped around him. Roop caught sight of a grey-skinned figure trickling through the flow of Earthers. He opened his mouth to call a greeting and doubled over.

"Oxygen!" he gasped.

A pair of grey hands pulled him upright. "What did you expect, idiot? Stand straight! If the Earthers think you're sick they'll quarantine you." The rebuke was hissed through closed teeth. "Keep your mouth shut 'til we get to the plant."

Roop trailed after him to the s-train. By the time they alighted the only other passengers were a few Vendonaxans and an Earther, whose energy seemed completely taken with the effort to breathe. He wore coveralls tucked into boots, and donned a mask and gloves before the doors opened at the stop for the chemical production compound.

"You can open your vents here," Roop's guide said.

They ascended to ground level and Roop took a deep relieved breath. Ahead was the goal of Roop's long journey hitching rides and stowing away: a sprawling complex of buildings wound about with pipes like intestines, wrapped in a mist of air so heavy that Roop felt he could cut it with the side of his hand.

"Beautiful!"

When news had reached Vendonax of Earth's ability to produce the life-giving carbons mon and bi that the alien bacteria had all but destroyed there, a rush had begun

99

by Vendonaxans eager to make their fortunes.

As they walked across the compound pocked with fluorescent puddles towards the low oblongs of the workers' quarters, Roop's guide began talking. "I'm Shookal. You'll share sleeping room with me. Avoid the Earthers where possible. Shouldn't be hard – they call us plant-rats. To them all this is waste, poison – and that makes those who work on it the lowest scum – tainted."

"But..." Roop was struggling to take in the sight of Vendonaxan children playing outside, running and shrieking with laughter without rasping coughs. Their skin was the glossy blue-grey of slate.

"Always remember – Earthers don't trust aliens and they always want a profit."

"What about those?" Roop turned back to look at a group of anti-contamination suited Earthers who had greeted them at the gate waving banners. There were several makeshift shelters nearby, enough for a small community no bigger than a litter of Vendonaxans.

"Especially stay away from them – they're dangerous!"

They had not looked dangerous to Roop. For a moment his eyes had met those of one of the Earthers, a female. They had looked at him the way his litter-mate had when he had left Vendonax, and she had stretched out her hand as if to prevent him entering as Shookal had pulled him on. Roop shrugged. He had been warned that everything on Earth was upside down.

Shookal opened the door to their sleeping room. "Unpack and get some rest. I'll be back when our shift starts.

The work was not difficult. The hard part was not letting the Earthers see how they did it. Roop and Shookal had to suit up to enter the heart of the plant. Their job was to monitor the stockpiles of waste and ensure there were no leaks. But there were leaks – everywhere. Roop hardly had to open his nose vents to detect them. Near each one, supposedly busy checking gauges or moving cylinders, was a Vendonaxan greedily inhaling.

"Shouldn't the faults be reported?"

Shookal gripped Roop's arm so hard that even through the suit it made him wince. "And what do you think the Earthers would do? Do you want to stop breathing?"

"If we told them the truth about Vendonax..."

Shookal's face blackened. "Tell anyone and you'll spend the rest of your days in quarantine breathing with your vents closed! While the company thinks it's exploiting us we're tolerated. If they discover we need their pollution, they'll make us sell Vendonax to pay for it."

Roop remembered the look in the Earther woman's eyes, but said nothing. Shookal placed him by a junction of pipes where the carbons almost formed a haze, and moved off to join two other Vendonaxans ostensibly checking the seals on row upon row of pressurized cylinders. They spoke in hisses impossible to distinguish above the hum of the chemical plant, but repeatedly cast looks in Roop's direction.

He soon gave up worrying about it in the ecstasy of inhaling freely. His starved body seemed to put out tendrils of healthy growth like a parched vine given water. The noises around him were twisted into abstract music and his head filled with colours. He saw the orange skies of Vendonax undistorted by the walls of the living pods, the deep slate colour of healthy Vendonaxan skin, the glow of fluorescent carbon-producing algae rimming the seashore.

He was shaken back to reality. Shookal thrust his face into Roop's. "Get outside and sober up – and walk straight!"

Roop nodded, setting lights swinging before his eyes. He tried to explain that long abstinence had caused him to lose his head for pure air, but his tongue did not seem to fit in his mouth. He stumbled outside where the taint of oxygen began to harden his euphoria into a headache. He forced his unruly limbs to take him on a walk around the perimeter. By the time he completed the circuit he should be steady enough to go back. Every few paces he had to pause.

"Are you all right?" It was the Earther woman from the gate. She gripped the fence as if she would shake it down.

Roop slumped against his side of it.

"The company treats you Vendonaxans shamefully. We're trying to help you."

"We could help ourselves if we worked together." Roop had seen how in his swirl of intoxicated visions.

"That's it – together we can close this place down!" The woman's fingers tightened on the fence.

"Close it down?" Roop was puzzled. "Vendonaxans could run it more efficiently." Play the Earthers at their own game; form a company; ship the waste back to Vendonax; turn the sky orange once more.

"It's poisoning you. Don't you see? And while you put up with it, it's poisoning Earth. You could help me expose what's going on here."

"You don't understand. We need to breathe..."

"Roop!" Shookal's voice dispersed the last fragments of light-headedness. "What did you tell her?" he demanded as soon as Roop was close enough not to be overheard. "Never mind." He cut off Roop's attempts to respond. "Go and sleep it off."

Sleep. The word alone made Roop feel better. He turned at the door to the living quarters, but Shookal was

102

no longer behind him. Instead, he was standing at the fence with the Earther woman. Sleep. All puzzles and plans could wait.

When Roop awoke the pounding behind his eyes had gone. He was ashamed; Shookal deserved his apology. He rose and went in search of him. One of the Vendonaxans in the canteen said he was working double time. Roop set off across the compound distracted by the children's games and the way the air seemed engaged in a sinuous dance with those moving through it. His attention was caught by a suited figure. An Earther near the Vendonaxan quarters? There was something in the way it moved, with a kind of conscious confidence. Despite Shookal's warning Roop approached.

"What are you doing here?"

The woman started. "Your friend showed me a way through the fence."

"Shookal did?"

"Yes. He's going to help me broadcast how the company abuses you." She raised her chin slightly so that Roop could see her throat microphone.

"Shookal is?" Roop felt like shaking his head to clear it.

"Yes. I'm to meet him in the storage area."

"I'll take you. I was looking for him anyway." He led the way into the plant, trying to check who was watching without looking as conspicuous as his companion. She began wheezing despite her mask as soon as they entered the enclosed work areas.

"How do you bear it?" she gasped.

Roop did not answer. Outside the storage area he stopped. There was a wonderful waft of carbons through the vent behind him. "In there," he said.

She looked puzzled.

"I'll keep watch." He quickly stepped out of sight as the door opened and closed behind her. Like everything else in the plant it did not seal properly and Roop could see inside where the lock had not caught. Shookal turned to meet her. His two workmates were attaching something to one of the pipes.

"Ah, Roop's friend." Shookal smiled at her and ripped her mask off. She doubled as if punched, her breath sounded as if it was being forced through pipes as leaky as the plant's. She tried to speak but sank to the floor.

"Here is your great chance to improve our lot," Shookal said.

Roop struggled not to cry out. He made himself look away from the Earther's distress to what the other Vendonaxans were doing. They had two vials of chemicals and some wires.

"When the protesters blow up the plant," Shookal said, "we Vendonaxans will have clean air all over Earth – of course, Earthers might find living here hard. I shouldn't wonder if we can demand anything we wish to restore the balance." He turned a remote ignition over and over in restless fingers as he spoke. He leaned closer to the woman so that she could taste his breath. "You say you want to help us, but you still shudder at our touch."

He straightened and jerked his head at his companions to leave. Roop leapt behind the door, waiting as they cleared the end of the corridor, but Shookal lingered bending over the woman.

"Don't worry, we'll make sure you get the credit."

Roop slid through the doorway behind him, took a deep breath of escaping carbons and raised one of the cylinders. The crack as it hit Shookal's head was followed by a thud as he crumpled onto the floor.

"Come." Roop dragged the Earther to the production floor, pushed her into the arms of a startled Vendonaxan and headed back. He reached the store room in time to see Shookal push himself onto an elbow. Then the ground shook and the building wavered as if in a heat haze.

Roop sat up in his hospital bed in the decontamination ward. The effects of absorbing so many pure chemicals and the sterile bubble in which he was being treated made him feel the explosion over again in his head. A nurse looked up, concerned. Roop would have liked to tell her that he was not about to die from the exposure he had suffered containing the sudden catastrophic overload in the chemical plant's systems, but that would have spoiled everything.

He and his co-workers, who had saved the plant from poisoning the swathe of Earth in the path of the prevailing wind, were being returned to Vendonax to spend their last days in the arms of their loved ones. Of course, as heroes their request for materials to set up their own plant on Vendonax was granted – especially as it meant Earth could ship its mess off-world. Vendonax would soon be self-sufficient in carbons again, and Roop would be the richest plant-rat in the galaxy.

**K.S. Dearsley**

K. S. Dearsley has an MA in Linguistics and Literature and has had numerous stories published on both sides of the Atlantic. She lives in Northampton, England, and is Writer in Residence at The Grid artists' studios in Warwickshire. Her fantasy novel, *Discord's Child*, is due to be published by Drollerie Press. Find out more at www.ksdearsley.com.

# Rosher Awakes

I lie here, looking at sky. It gives me my bearings. Although it changes; clouds, clear blue, rainy streaks, darkness, moonlight, the changes are comprehensible. I turn to it in relief from this mishmash of colours and shapes around me, all blending into each other, where nothing has clear definition. I hear sounds as if from under water, separated from any meaning. If I fix my gaze on it, the sky, always familiar, allows me to stay awake. Otherwise, churning panic at this strangeness takes over and although I try not to draw attention, cries escape from my mouth. Then someone comes over and touches me saying, "Rosher, Rosher", whatever that means. Then I fall asleep. They do that. They touch, then sleep comes again.

Sometimes I emerge from dreaming expecting familiar surroundings, but no, always the same strange sights seeming out of focus somehow. I have learned to begin by looking at sky, then to progress downwards to –can I call it a window frame since it has no edges? Then a transparency of wall, and, lower, a lump of me under some light trappings that might be bandages, so I'm in a bed, but the rest of it? Is this a wall? Is that a wall opposite? How can it be if it is so transparent, with people walking through it without obvious doorways?

I felt proud today, proud that I managed to look at the whole room, if it can be called a room, even the most frightening parts, without wincing and crying out. There is a kind of presence, but not really solid – I think of it as a ghost/giant. It appears suddenly in the centre of this space and speaks. People – normal sized people – stand still and listen to it, then as soon as it disappears they rush off in different directions.

But more frightening are those other presences. They

seem to be sleeping heads, suspended in the air, not moving, just breathing, though occasionally twitching slightly. They are in a row with a gap in the middle and seem not to be attached to anything. That's what bothers me; the stuff of nightmares, floating sleeping heads. I take refuge again in the sky.

I woke remembering. There had been a bit of heart trouble; nothing major, but Fairfield Hospital admitted me for tests. I had a very bad night; trying to call out for help; pain; blackouts. That is all I can recall before waking here. But wherever are Sal and the boys? Surely they must have been informed of my transfer. I cried out, "Sal, Sal" but nobody understood. They touched me and I slept again.

Feeling slightly better I have begun to look through the *window* down from the skyscape to the shapes beneath it; shapes which must I think be buildings, but so unfamiliar I cannot work out the perspective. Are they close to this place and quite small, or far away and huge? I had thought I was imagining a disturbing change of shape and colour, but now it seems as if they are rotating very slowly. Sometimes there is a shimmering of reflected light. Maybe I was transferred to a foreign hospital, too far away for Sal and the boys to stay for a long period. The nurses' physique is puzzling. They seem to be a different race, tall with elongated heads and supple, wavy arms. I can't place them. Are they double-jointed? They seem to flow, not stride.

From a distance the language sounds like English, but when they come near I can make nothing of it. They say "Eed" when they feed me, "Gerink" when they give me a drink. "Aham" is *yes*, "Na na" is *No*. What language could that be?

They have put me on solid food now, allowing me to feed myself. I have never been one to turn down a good meal,

107

even if the taste is unidentifiable and it comes in a bowl the size of an orange. They fill it up pretty frequently, though.

I solved two mysteries at once yesterday. The window is definitely a window as I discovered by accidentally leaning on something by the bed that operated it. A second later water came cascading in, scattering a few leaves over me. There was a flurry of activity, nurses saying, "Rosher, Rosher," with tut-tutting sounds as the *window* was closed again and the bed spontaneously dried itself.

The second mystery – the buildings with a green side have plants growing up their vertical surfaces. This hospital is one of them. They rotate, at times turning their living sides to the sun, or, in the midday heat, turning them away as water showers down causing the shimmering effect. Unluckily for me I leaned on the opening device just as the *rain* came.

Pleased with my discovery yesterday, and trying to make amends to the nurses for the rain shower, I said, "Eed" before they gave me the bowl, and "Gerink" as my drink appeared. What a flurry! One of the ghost/giants materialised in the middle of the room, smiling. The nurses looked very pleased with themselves. Of course! The ghost/giants must be images of their superiors, communicating with them in a more sophisticated way than appearing on a screen. In spite of their superhuman size, they look absolutely real.

This boss said "Eed" and a food bowl appeared in his hand, then "Gerink" and a liquid container followed. Dogs, cats, trees and hosts of unknown objects appeared as he spoke each word distinctly, producing them like a conjurer. This was a language lesson, I decided, but why?

Their patient does not intend staying for a long period; he proved to be rather an inept pupil, remembering only "gog", "cad" and "deree".

I woke suddenly in the night after a dream, still vivid, still real. I was setting out for my club, the *Second Life Society*, and Sal was telling the boys never to go with me to "that group of fanatics." It was unnatural she always said, people wanting their bodies preserved for posterity. I used to tell her she was behind the times, that she should read the American magazines. At the club we devoured every article. And of course we all went in for that famous competition; first prize – after death the full works, even the funeral paid for. I took time tourism as my theme; for me the chance to see new developments; fascinating changes; for *future friends* as I chose to call them the advantage would be conversations with living history. Me.

Such astonishment when old Roger Entwistle from Brandlesholme won. Sal, quiet, upset, a believer all her life, objected till they flew us to America. She prayed in the chapel at the complex. The priest promised a real funeral with the words *in the sure and certain hope of the resurrection*. There was to be no euthanasia. After a natural death my body would be sent to America. So she agreed. We signed.

Still half in the dream, looking out at the black sky, at the moon with its cold, grey mountains, I realised. That last blackout, when I went into hospital for tests, was the end. I must have had a heart attack then, and died. So they had held a funeral, mourned me. The moon, the vast distances on such an inhuman scale reminded me that Sal and the boys were as far away. They must have died cold years, perhaps centuries ago. My eyes filled with tears for them. I wanted to run from this nightmare; think of them

109

in solitude. But involuntarily I sobbed. "Rosher, Rosher". They touched me and I slept again.

The day after realisation struck, a feeling of sick hollowness caused me to push food away; I even threw the bowl across the room. It sailed right through a ghost/giant, causing consternation amongst the subservient nurses.

"They are more real than you," I yelled as they twittered over me. "Sal and the boys, they are here, now, here and here." I pointed to my head, my heart. "None of this nonsense is real." I turned my face from them. A nurse came to touch me. As I was drifting into sleep I heard "Rosher Enderwizu" and I realised she was trying to say my name.

There is no point in retreating into sleep, memories or imaginings. After what may have been weeks of escapism, the realisation dawns upon me that this is my situation and I have to deal with it. So I shall try to understand as much as possible about being here.

First, the language that sounds like English. It is English, isn't it? But how much time elapsed to change it so much? And the *double-jointed* race? Have they evolved to a further stage? What powers do they have that I don't?

Whilst I was dreaming and fantasizing about my real life, as opposed to this nightmare existence, they left me alone. But now, sensing a change of attitude they keep coming over and encouraging me to look around, especially at the floating, sleeping heads that I try not to see. Occasionally there seems to be a kind of notice, something in code under each one, but I can make nothing of it. At other times, the heads seem lower, and there is no code. I look at them and shrug. The nurses giggle as if sharing a secret hidden from me.

The ghost/giant, the self-appointed language teacher appears more often now. He is giving me lots of word labels but nothing to help me express what I want or feel. I humour him though. Hardest to remember are words for things I don't really understand, like sleeping heads, wall/door transparency or that touch to make people sleep.

Yesterday they undressed me. My mind lurched, refusing to accept what my eyes insisted on. I closed them again, opening them again slowly. Shock, disbelief. Where were my arthritic shoulders, creaky hips? What was this young, fresh tissue with flowing, elongated limbs? Elongated, but much smaller than they should be. What have they done? Given me a child's body; made me into a *hybrid*, to look like one of their own? As the nurses washed me I thought, "No mirror. Please, no mirror." I could not bear to see my eyes, the eyes of an old man mourning wife and sons, looking out of a child's face.

Something has happened to the sleeping heads. Suddenly this morning the one to the right of that space in the middle began to twitch violently, as if having some kind of seizure. Then the eyes opened, staring round in what looked like frantic disbelief.

"Atta, Atta," called a nurse and they all ran through the wall in the same direction. A long finger appeared next to the face, touching it until the eyes closed.

Of course! The sleeping heads are each an image on a monitor, so that even when working in another part of the hospital, the nurses can keep an eye on these special patients. What had prevented me from understanding this simple fact was that the screens, like everything else here have no edges; they blend in with their surroundings.

Then the heads disappeared. The monitors must have

been switched off. For a long time no nurses appeared and I began to grow restless, never having been left alone before.

I was drifting off into a daydream about the lupins and hollyhocks in my garden at Brandlesholme when suddenly the heads appeared again, but slightly higher than before. That *code* beneath each was now revealed to be a name. Previously I must have been looking at the tops of letters on each label.

I searched for the distorted face. It was missing, but there under the gap was the name *Anita Smith*. To my astonishment the other gap, the one in the middle, was labelled *Roger Entwwistle*. Had Anita, 'Atta', as they called her, been transferred somewhere else? Or had the shock of waking been too traumatic... Had the nurses done the humane thing? The others, David Willis, Patrick Henderson, Ann Joliffe and Christine Edwards went on sleeping peacefully as the monitors were re-adjusted and their names disappeared.

They spruced me up today, fussing and twittering around me like anxious birds. Instead of the usual white robe I was dressed in vivid blue, with a kind of magnetic badge attached to the front. I amused the nurses and myself by pulling it off and letting it find its way back to my chest.

Then a woman came in with a man behind her. Hesitating, she sat beside me and pronounced slowly and laboriously, "How-you-do-pleased-meet-you."

I gasped.

"Who are you? Why am I here? Tell me what all this is about."

She looked blank, then, "Pleased-meet-your-acquaintance."

So they were only phrases, learned parrot fashion. I

was disappointed, but she took my hand and tried once more. "How-you-are-keeping-well?"

For the first time in this endless nightmare, someone had asked me how I felt.

"No!" I shouted. "No, no!" My eyes filled with tears. She started caressing me and I pulled away indignantly, thinking of Sal. But of course this woman saw me as a child. Crestfallen she turned to the man.

Feeling churlish, and beginning to intuit who she was, I tried to make amends by pointing to my food bowl and saying "eed". They responded with smiles, so I put myself through my paces, repeating the vocabulary of the language lessons.

"Good male... na, na... good boy," she said with a smile.

Later, awake in the night, staring at the moon again, I shivered. Sal was right, as ever. I had had a naïve dream of time tourism – tourism! Tourists normally return home to a safe envelope of familiar contexts; bore their family, friends, neighbours with souvenirs and recollections. They are not marooned in such a foreign place as this for ever.

What do these people want of me? To live amongst them, a child with a life lived inside me? Was that woman a historian, a researcher? Certainly from her attempts at twentieth century English I gather she is no linguist. Also her manner, kind and reassuring, revealed that she loved children. The whole atmosphere; excited preparation; her affectionate caresses, all this had the feel of an adoption meeting rather than a research interview.

I wonder, did she read my competition entry, and choose me to be woken? Am I to have interesting conversations with her, my new Mother?

Yet she has been the only person since I opened my

eyes to ask me how I feel. If I am to express to these people even a small fraction of my suffering, it will have to be through her.

Sal was right to have her doubts. Right as usual. Deep in my mind the decision forms, cold, hard as that distant moon. Death is as natural as life; clean, clear, comprehensible, unlike this grotesque tangle. I shall learn enough *New English* to plead with her: "Please, pity me. Give me back my death."

**Shirley Percy**

Shirley Percy is a retired ethnic minority achievement support teacher. She thoroughly enjoyed her 36 years in Primary school but found that they left little time for other pursuits. Nowadays she loves writing and is an enthusiastic member of "Womanswrite". She has recently had a poem *Raymond* published in *Best of Manchester Poets*. She is a Buddhist and lives in Bury with a husband and three ex-stray cats.

# The Green Run

## Chapter 1

Sitting on the worn hotel settee Tyler's blue eyes examine the foyer. "Just relax Rang, everything will be fine."

Rang stands at the window, angular features taut and expressionless, her grey eyes moving from the grey Mersey sky to look over every nook and cranny of the room. "I don't like this place, dirty shit holes like this should be levelled."

Tyler lifts the trilby from his head, a ponytail of jet-black hair cascading down. "Do ya wanna keep your voice down for god's sake, the fella's only in the next fucking room? Listen, it's got four walls and a roof. We can use it then, right?" Silence descends between them, the only noise the buzzing of the reception computer terminal and the passing traffic.

A sneer stretches across her cherry red lips, her eyes moving back to the battered black Ford Interceptor in the car park. "This is important, I'm supposed to be keeping you alive and you pick this karsey."

"DiamondBlue said it's a good place to lay low and if he recommends it, then it must be safe."

Rang shakes her long Alban ringlets. "Now look who's opening their mouth?" Her voice pitches to Tyler's tone. "Do ya wanna keep your voice down for god's sake, the fella's only..."

"Yeah yeah, all right. You made your point you dumb bit..." His voice trails off as footsteps echo from the corridor behind the reception desk.

From round the corner a portly middle-aged man, wrapped in an ill-fitting, frayed and food stained brown suit, moves to the reception desk. "Now sir, I'm sorry to have kept you both waiting like that, the computer's having trouble with your identity card Mr Pennington. I just need to confirm your first name is Brice, correct?"

Tyler stands, straightening the jacket of his mottled grey suit, his hawkish nose twitching as he moves with purposeful steps to the desk. "Yes that's right."

"If you could swipe your chip across the scanner?" Smiling, Tyler leans over, brushing the knuckles of his left hand across the metal plate. The man smiles back. "It will just take a few seconds sir." His yellow-toothed smile changes, his leg swinging under the desk, foot impacting metal. Rang spins round, moving a couple of steps towards the slum lord, eyes burning a hole through him. His eyes move to meet hers, stepping sideways a concrete smile instantly jumping to his face. "I'm sorry for the delay, as I said we're having a bit of trouble with the computer. Won't take too long."

Tyler nods, beads of sweat forming on his heavily bronzed forehead. "That's all right..." He pauses, voice pitching so high only dogs can hear it. Coughing, his voice returns to normal. "Excuse me! That's fine."

Rang brushes her long, thin fingers over her hip. "I'll get our bags."

The slum lord taps the computer terminal, his brown eyes flitting from Rang walking out the door, to Tyler and back. "Nearly finished Mr Pennington. The terminal in each room can organise for alarm calls, maps, places of interest and route planners if you need them." He pulls the door cards from the printer, coughing violently over the hand holding them before placing both on the desk. "That's rooms eighteen and twenty-four. There are your keys, your complimentary gifts will be sent up in the morning. Will there be anything else?"

116

Tyler shakes his head. Reaching for them he hesitates, momentarily slipping on a pair of black gloves before picking the cards up, placing them in his pocket. "Errrrr, thank you. I think?" The slum lord nods, craning to see Rang through the window he moves back down the corridor. Watching the man leave, Tyler turns his attention to the grime-covered window, Rang's form obscured by the open boot while pulling out two large sports bags. He walks to the door, his voice barely audible. "OK Diamond Blue, you'd better be right."

Dropping both bags to the floor Rang moves to the doorway, listening against the outside. Armalite 12mm in hand she opens the door, moving inside her eyes scan the room. "All right, bring the stuff in."

Tyler picks the bags up, carrying them into the room as Rang moves to the window, pulling down the shutter.

Placing both bags on the nearest twin bed Tyler moves to look around. "You see it's not that bad is it? Just for tonight?"

Rang steps into the bathroom, checking the shower cubicle. "That's your opinion." She sniffs. "What's that smell? It's like something's died in here and left a little reminder."

Tyler places one of the bags on the floor, moving to the window he pulls the shutters back, gazing into the night's sky. "We could always try the other room. Tell me again why we got two rooms?"

Rang walks out of the bathroom, inspecting the door lock she turns to see Tyler at the window. "Get away from the window, idiot." Walking over she grabs him by the collar, pulling him away. "The other room's a precaution. Anyone who comes for us will have to make a choice which room you're in, this one or the other. To solve the problem they'll have to either split up or chance

117

their luck. Evens up they'll get it wrong, as long as we're quiet."

"Just seems a waste, all that money gone."

"You can always sleep there on your own? I'm sure your ex-employer would love you to. Why don't we just give him a ring to find out?"

The colour drains from Tyler's face. "Ammm! No it's OK." Curling up fully clothed on the bed he pulls a pillow from under the sheets.

Rang moves to the chair, removing her jacket and throwing it onto the empty bed, straightening her dark red jump suit. Rummaging inside the bag on the floor she pulls out a magazine, various cars on the cover. "Just get some sleep for my sake, I'll sit here and keep watch."

"The door." Rang moves out of the chair to the wall, gun in hand.

Tyler crouches behind the bed. "No-one should be here. They must have found us."

"Damn slum lord. Let's find out." Levelling the gun at the door, shot after shot rings out. A thud echoes outside, the groaning slowly drifting into silence.

"Emmm, sorry. Just remembered, that could be my complimentary breakfast."

Rang breathes in deep as the alleyway looms far below. The rattle of the rusted fire escape making her heart jump in her chest, the weight of two bags pulling her towards the ground. "Why do I have to go down first?"

Tyler shakes his head. "Because you're the one who shot through the door, you could have waited but noooo! Take a backbone pill for god's sake, anyway it's not that far."

"We're on the fourth floor; you cling to this rickety thing and say that."

"I... I... I would but I'm allergic to heights." Tyler's nose twitches.

"Don't you mean you're scared of heights?"

"No I'm allergic to height; I come out in a terrible rash. Iron as well, terrible rash all over my body."

Rang squints through her black eyeliner, cocking her head to the side. "You've never told me that!"

Tyler nods his head. "Yep, yep, very bad. That's why I can't play golf, you know, the irons."

"Is that being allergic to iron?"

"Yes it is, that's how it works."

"That makes no sense, how are you going to get down? Anyway, are golf clubs made of iron? I mean they'd begin to..."

"Now listen here, I'm a corporate executive. Years of private schools, Oxford University, graduated with honours, I know what I'm talking about. You! You're a nomad and a grunt at that. May I remind you at the moment you're working for me? Get down there! I'll climb down in a minute and meet you at the car, OK?"

"I guess so, sir." Rang begins to descend, stopping momentarily to speak before shaking her head and continuing down. Moving back into the room Tyler kneels at the slum lord's body, red tracks tracing the path back to the door. Searching the body his hand closes round the man's wallet. Pulling it out, he examines the contents, empty except for numerous fifty pound notes and a piece of paper the name Pennington scrawled in pencil on the outside. Opening the paper, Tyler screws his eyes up trying to read the words. Shaking his head he places the paper into his pocket. Moving to the window a screech of twisting metal drifts from outside, the crescendo of sound ending with a cry and thud. Tyler leans out, eyes searching for Rang, the ladder now swinging at an odd angle to the wall.

Below, lying on the lid of a large dumpster, Rang stares into the sky. The thick plastic lid bevelled and ripped underneath her. She pushes against the lip of the receptacle, trying to free herself from the hole in the cover. She looks up at him and growls, "There, are you happy now? I'm lying in garbage. If that's a rat nudging my backside I'm going to feed him to you."

Tyler waves his hand away from his body. "Yeah yeah, whatever, just hurry up and check the perimeter, I'll be down soon." Moving to the door he places his ear to the wood, the hallway as quiet as a graveyard in the dead of night. Pulling the gun from inside his coat he slowly tugs the door open, slipping into the hallway. Barrel pointing down the empty corridor he slowly sweeps the weapon from left to right, his eyes scanning every entrance along both walls. He stalks into the hallway, slow delicate steps as he reaches the end of the corridor. Opening the door he steps through, checking the stairwell. Back against the wall, the wooden stairs creak under the weight of each step down. The aroma of each landing invades his nostrils, the smell of sawdust and urine stronger than he remembered.

Reaching the ground floor, he places his ear to the exit leading into the foyer, the low buzz of the main desk computer terminal overwhelming everything. Opening the door he tucks the gun under his trench coat, the barrel resting against the small of his back. Into the foyer he rounds the front desk to check the computer, glancing down the corridor into the back room. Moving into the office he scans the room, the CCTV screen jumping between the reception, stairwell, and numerous corridors.

On the wall, rows and rows of stained storage units hold small blue disks in transparent cases. Running his finger down the rack he pulls out yesterday and today's disks, stuffing them into his coat pocket and ejecting the disk from the recorder.

A voice says, "Hello." Turning round Tyler levels his gun, spitting lead from the muzzle, punching pool-ball sized holes into the plasterboard wall. He stops, eyes scanning the room, his pulse racing like a steam train. "Heluuuurrrr! Wi Luv roo, roo Luv re, reaa a harrr..." The voice dies out, the head of the furry dinosaur alarm clock sitting on the shelf in bits on the floor.

Tyler smiles, placing the disk from the recorder into his coat pocket. "Fuck you Barney, Grimlock rules." Levelling the gun he fires again, the clock exploding into a cloud of purple plastic. He pushes a pen drive into the port of the computer stack, clicking a small button on the stick. The computer springs into life, the background of palm trees and sand on the monitor dissolving into a black digital haze. Walking to the door he levels the gun, sending three shots smashing into the computer and disk player, both machines erupting to a shower of metal and plastic. Reaching just below his ear he presses against the skin. "Everything's clear in here, get prepared, we're checking out of this place."

## Chapter 2

Moving out of the hotel's front door Tyler grimaces, placing his hand over his eyes to block the sun. Rummaging in his leather trench coat he pulls out a pair of mirrored sunglasses. He moves towards the Interceptor, the whole chassis rocking back and forth to the rumble of the engine. Rang stands up from sitting on the bonnet.

"Did you get everything?"

Tyler lifts his hand, palm facing Rang. "Yeah yeah yeah, got the tapes from the camera and downloaded the virus into the hotel's server. Good luck to anyone who tries to recover that. What are you waiting for? Get in."

Rang shakes her head. "No, you're driving. If we do meet trouble, I want my hands free. I've put the supplies in the compartment under the boot, and the package on top."

"I checked the slum lord and he had this on him," said Tyler, passing Rang the piece of paper. "What do you think?"

Rang scans the paper. "If this is the address let's get it over with, bargaining's gonna be like ice-skating up a hill. Ya think the grubby bastard sold us out?"

Tyler smiles. "That's the billion dollar question isn't it? Let's face it this is going to get rough."

"Can you handle it?"

"What do you mean?"

"I mean it's going to get messy, I need to know you're not gonna turn into a mound of blubbering jelly. Remember, we're about to deal with one of the nastiest operators in the Liverpool conurbation."

Tyler waves her off while moving to the driver's door, opening it he steps inside. "Look, we've worked together before, you have to learn to trust me. I'll be fine, I've got it all planned." Leaning down he moves into the driver's seat. A dull thud rings through the air, Tyler's head hitting the door frame.

Staring at Tyler she shakes her head. "Yes sir." Rang moves round to the open passenger door. Taking her coat off she throws it into the back, placing her gun under the passenger seat. "Can you drive?"

Clutching his temple he nods. Placing the sedan in

122

reverse he pulls out of the parking space, through the car park and into the streets. Rummaging in his pocket he pulls out the slum lord's wallet. "Here, look through that and see if there's anything of use."

Taking the wallet Rang starts to empty the contents, she stops. "There's no money in this."

Tyler lets out a long slow breath, eyes still locked on the road. "Oh really, that's a shame."

"There was no money in it?"

He shrugs, nose twitching like a mouse with cheese. "You've got it, you tell me."

"Come on, come on, stop messing around."

"I don't know what you mean."

Rang clicks her fingers. "Bullshit! How much was in there?"

His nose shudders again. "Don't know what you're talking about, it was like that when I found it."

"So this slum lord, in his own place and with a till somewhere, doesn't have any money in his wallet. Is that what you're trying to tell me?"

Turning the wheel at the corner Tyler shakes his head, his nose twitching. "I guess so. Maybe he spent it or left it in the office." Rang shakes her head, gazing out to the passing streets and the cabin falls silent. Tyler looks over, Rang's aura chilling his skin. "Shall we take Netherton Way or Church Road?" Rang remains silent, a barely audible exhale escaping her lips. "If we take Netherton we're going through Fifth Ring gang territory, if we take Church Road, and then past the dock we're into the Street Masks area. What do you think?" Silence. "Netherton will get us to the tunnel quicker but the Fifth lot don't like people through their territory." The air within the cabin was a vast whistling ice glacier. "Are we not talking?" Rang scratches her slender porcelain neck.

Tyler waves at her. "Why am I the last to know things like this?"

"I don't know, because you're a moron. Because you're a liar and a thief."

"Not sure that has anything to do with it. Hold on, what makes you think I'm a liar?"

Rang turns to look at him. "You know, all this time we have worked together it's the first time I've noticed it."

Slowing the car his eyes flit from the road, to Rang, then back. "Noticed what?"

"Your tell."

"My what?"

"I can tell when you're lying to me, you lied on the ladder and you're doing it now. The slum lord had money and you've palmed it."

Looking her straight in the eyes he shakes his head. "Honestly, I don't know what you're talking about." His nose starts to jerk.

"In poker some players have subconscious mannerisms that give them away when they're bluffing. If you know what to look for then you have an advantage. Yours is the twitch of your beak."

Tyler places one hand over his nose, feeling round, his hand flies back to the wheel as the alloys knock against the kerb. He sighs, mouthing under his breath. "No wonder I always lose in the casinos."

Clicking her fingers Rang extends her hand. "Come on, come on. Give me my share!"

"He didn't have much, a couple of twenties and the note." He covers his face with his hand, scratching his nose.

"What, do you think I'm dumb or something? It's even more obvious now, give me your wallet."

"There's nothing in there."

Rang extends her hand further. "Then you won't mind me taking it then?"

Shaking his head his hand moves back to the steering wheel. "Yes I would! My wallet is very personal. How would you like me to go through your bag? I bet there's stuff in there that's important?"

"There isn't anything in my bag that important, now give me the money."

"There's just a couple of twenties, nothing special..." Tyler's voice drifts off, eyes fixing on something through the rear view mirror. "What's that?"

Rang raises an eyebrow, head scanning from side to side. "What? What am I looking for?"

"No, not out there, behind us."

Twisting around she scans the dual carriageway, eyes moving across the buildings from left to right, then to the road. "What? I can't see anything except buildings and the empty road..." Her voice trails off, eyes squinting for focus. "I'm not sure, that looks like a box or something in the road."

"Yes, my concern is it's starting to catch us up."

"What? Don't be absurd. It's just a shoe box." Squinting her eyes again she takes a deep breath. "That doesn't seem to be going away, oh shit."

Tyler squeezes on the wheel, sitting upright in the chair as if it was wired for shock treatment. "What is it?"

Rang turns back round, pulling her 12mm from under the seat. "Listen. Whatever you do don't let it catch us."

"Why?"

Reaching for the electric window the glass retracts. "Because it's following us, I've just seen some flashing lights and we have no idea what's inside."

"What could be inside?"

"At this point I don't really think it's flowers and

125

chocolates, Interflora don't usually deliver in such an unusual way do they? Lose it."

Tyler pushes down on the throttle, the whirl of the supercharger kicking in. The Interceptor surges forward, squeezing in between two cars to its right, passing within millimetres of the back bumper of one and front headlight of the other. The vehicle behind him screeches, swerving to the right almost into the lane of oncoming traffic. Rang grabs the hand hold just above the passenger door. Her left hand drops the gun into her lap, feeling for the belt release. "Jesus man, that was close."

Tyler shakes his head, vision bolted to the tarmac ahead. "That was nothing, you should have been in this seat."

Rang looks back, box swerving right and out of sight behind an automobile. "I've lost it, can't see it anymore."

"Lean out of the window, try and get a fix."

"The way you drive I'll be tumbling down the road."

"I need to know where it is for hell's sake, to keep ahead of it!"

Climbing through the passenger window she stretches out, sitting on the closed car door. Her feet hanging onto the under edge of her seat, hand grasping the rail under the window. Craning her neck she sees something white and fast races from besides a hatchback, accelerating between the right wheels of a green saloon and the central reservation. Rang moves back into the passenger seat. "Hit the brakes, cause the traffic behind to swerve." A screech and the Interceptor decelerates. The lane of traffic ripples, trucks and compacts changing direction as the effect hits the green saloon. The vehicle swerves right, pushing the box into the grass of the central reservation. The box hits a stone, ricochets into the air and over the back of the vehicle, smashing into the road. A high pitched whirr and the box explodes with a thunderous roar. Waves of pressure reverberate through the Interceptor. Vehicles in the area deflect off the force of the blast, veering into the breakdown lane and sidings. Cars swerve and lurch, crashing into cannonballs of twisting, screeching metal. A distant red Munich saloon drifts into view, tyres digging into the now hazy left hand lane, far behind the dance of shimmering wreckage. Swerving between vehicle fragments, a red wing whistling past the right side of the Munich.

Pulling herself back through the passenger window Rang rummages in her pocket, breathing deeply as her fingers caress her spare clip. "Jesus, those things are lethal. Get this bloody thing moving for hell's sake!"

"I'm flooring it, I'm flooring it."


## Chapter 3

The smoke and wreckage shrinks into the distance, the Munich gathering ground on the Interceptor. A red four-by-four glides sideways behind the Interceptor, through the outside lane and over the metal railing of the junction to the road below.

The saloon gains speed as the Interceptor runs across and down the slip road. Jerking backwards with a shudder, the Munich cutting over the grass verge in pursuit. Tyler moves the Ford through the lights, taking a sharp left turn. The saloon, riding close behind surges forth, smashing its bull bars into the back of the Interceptor. The Interceptor jerks, the sound of twisting metal and wailing tyres fill the cabin. Tyler checks the rear view mirror, the light of the sun reflecting off the car's bonnet and dark tinted windows. The Munich smashes into the back, the Ford swerving and weaving all over the road. A vague shadow moves in the passenger side of the car, flecks of sunlight piercing through the front passenger window. An arm reaches through, a shape of glistening metal in hand. Shots ring out, one bullet after another slamming into the boot lid and passenger door of the Interceptor. Rang grabs her gun. "Little fuckers, look what they've done to my car."

Tyler shakes his head. "Is that all you're bloody worried about?"

"Hey! It took me six months to find this car and all I could get was a replica, and now look at it!" Pulling her body through the window she extends her arm, firing round after round at the saloon. Bullets ricochet off the reinforced front wing, others punching large dents in the rear driver's door.

The Munich skids, crossing into the oncoming lane before gaining control. An oncoming car swerves, veering onto the pavement and smashing headlong into a graffiti-covered brick wall. A second car skids anti-clockwise, the edge narrowly missing the back of the Interceptor. Tyler turns left, wheels bouncing onto the pavement and over an old public waste bin. The bin clatters underneath, moving down the chassis and out across into the road. Rang, still leaning out of the car, jams her feet under the passenger side of the dashboard, legs and back twisting at an uncomfortable angle. The knuckles of her left hand white on the passenger door handle, right hand wafting, empty of a weapon. Pulling herself back inside Rang grasps her leg. "Jesus Tyler, that was too close for comfort."

Tyler pulls the Ford right, regaining the firm grip on the pot hole ridden surface of the road. Through the side window his eyes catch the fast approaching saloon, on collision course for the driver's side. "Hold on!" Dumping the clutch the Interceptor jerks forward, Tyler's foot burying the accelerator deep into the foot well. Both cars connect with a screech of metal, the Munich smashing sidelong into the Ford. The tyres of both cars wail with mistreatment, the deflection veering both into the opposite lane. Tyler turns the wheel, correcting the slide and smashing into the headlight of the Munich, deflecting it into a full spin.

Rang reaches under the passenger part of the dashboard. Compartment opening to reveal another gleaming 12 mm. Pulling the gun from the hollow she checks the weapon clip. "What are they doing?!"

Looking in the rear view mirror Tyler shakes his head. "They've just hit the kerb but are starting to move again." Tyler turns down a small side road, accelerating quickly through the gears, the distant rumble of the Munich in his ears. Rang leans out of the passenger window, bracing her back against the inside of the door. She fires, one round missing, the second smashing into the Munich's broken front wing. A hand stretches from the front passenger seat, resting on the side mirror. Fire and light flash from the muzzle, a chorus of clangs reverberating through the rear of the Interceptor. An explosive hiss passes through the car, back swerving from left to right, a dull thudding and scraping of metal through the chassis.

"Shit," says Tyler, "they've hit the tyres, hang on."

Rang sits back in the chair, reaching for her seatbelt. The car swerves, Tyler's hands white with the effort to correct the wheels. The back swings left, the sparking rear wheel deflecting off the kerb, pushing violently right. Tyler shifts the wheel savagely, slamming his foot on the breaks to no avail. The car skids, the edge of the driver's side heads first through a thin brick wall as the back spins anti-clockwise. Tyler pulls on the steering wheel, slowing the spin into a drift, the car shuddering to a halt in the broken field of the concrete.

Rang slumps back in the seat clutching her neck and shoulder under the seat belt. "Damn it, my arm." Unhooking the belt she fumbles in the passenger foot well, the cold metal of the gun slowing her heartbeat. "Tyler you still with me?" She pulls the passenger handle, the relatively untouched door swinging open.

Tyler shakes his head, blood trickling down his chin from a fibrous cut in his Dermamesh woven skin. "Yeah, I'll live." Trying the door, to no avail, he climbs into the passenger seat.

Pulling the boot open Rang lifts the black box from the car, placing it in a dark gray cricket hold-all. Lifting a portion of the false boot she grabs an MP7, throwing it to Tyler along with a few clips, grabbing another for herself. "Listen, I can still hear the car. Can you see any way out of here?"

Tyler scans the compound. "There's an alleyway over there, turns left but can't see anything else."

Both drop into cover behind the Ford, the Munich screeching to a halt just outside the collapsed wall. The passenger door opens as a man steps out, wearing a multicoloured sleeveless V neck shirt and hockey mask. Ducking his long silver hair under the line of the window, he moves to the back of the car, springing up into a firing position, his gun resting on the boot lid. The driver scrambles out of the passenger door, falling into a heap below the window line and out of sight. His shadow moves with fidgeting speed to the front of the car, positioning himself to lean on the bonnet, balaclava masking his face. They fire, more rounds streaming into the compound, hot lead piercing the side of the Interceptor. "All right, come on out. We can see ya moving behind there."

Tyler clicks a magazine into the MP7. "Well, what do we do now?"

Taking a deep breath Rang exhales slowly. "I'm thinking, I'm thinking." The air grows silent for a breath, then more rounds. Her eyes sparkle. Reaching into the back of the car she pulls the seat down. Fumbling under the false boot she extracts two clips, orange marker scribbled either side. "I've got an idea, and these High Explosive Armour-Piercing shells should do the trick." A smile creeps across her face. Looking up and to the left Tyler swallows hard. "Oh god, you've got that look on your face again."

"What look?"

"That screams to me I need better medical insurance."

She shakes her head. "You're so jittery sometimes. Now listen! I want you to surrender."

Tyler rubs his ear, shaking his head like he's just come out of the water. "I'm sorry, WHAT?"

"I need their attention focused on you."

"Oh well, thanks for that."

Putting her hand up, finger pointing to the sky Rang grunts. "Look, I haven't got time to explain. Now can you do it or not?"

Stopping in mid breath he sighs. "I guess so, but I could die!"

"Surrender." Rang expels the clip from her 12mm, slamming in the HEAP clip.

"Errrm, OK." Another hail of bullets ricochets around them.

Falling onto her back she motions in their direction. "Look, I'm dead, one of the last bullets got through. Surrender, take ten paces then hit the ground."

Tyler swallows hard. Turning, he places his hands in the air, dropping his gun. "I surrender, I surrender."

The man in the balaclava scans the Interceptor.

"Where's your friend?"

Tyler shakes his head. "She's dead you bastard."

Standing up, the balaclava man cranes his neck, his white shirt and gray leather jacket wafting in the breeze. "Where's the box, that's all we're after. Your ex-employer wants his property back."

"It's here." Tyler lifts the bag onto the bonnet of the car.

"Bring it here and no funny business."

With a last look Tyler trudges round the car. One step. Two steps. Three. Four. Shoes crunching on the rough gravel ground. Five. Six. Seven. The ice hockey man slowly steps round the car. Eight. Nine. From under the Interceptor Rang levels her pistol at the Munich. Ten. Pumping rounds through the back wing, punching fist sized holes into the petrol tank. The back explodes, showers of twisted metal cascade in every direction, engulfing the car in flames. Screams echo from nearby, the ice hockey man thrown headlong, three car lengths down the street. The man in the balaclava cries in pain, thrown backwards into the wall of a derelict warehouse, sliding into a heap on the floor.

Standing up Tyler shakes his head, legs trembling underneath his body weight. His eyes scan the wreckage. "Wow!"

Rang stands, moving quickly to the boot, rummaging in the secret compartment for more clips and her sword. "Hey. Tyler! Wake up! We need to go. Now!"

## Chapter 4

Moving through the side doors Rang surveys the area, the bright florescent light reflecting off the scarred white and black vein stone floor. The dull buzz of kiosk signs drifts through the hazy station air. "The area's secure and I'm in position."

A form steps through the front doors, trench coat hood enveloping his face. "Where's the network centre?"

Rang glances towards the unit to her right. "It's over there, near the information office."

Walking towards the office Tyler veers off into a room of dappled green, the walls either side honeycombed with flat screen terminals. In the back wall, columns of doors the size of oil drums stack one by one on top of another. From above, a mechanical arm dislodges from a nook in the roof. The dull, slightly tarnished alloy descends, unfurling a square horizontal platform, moving into position below one of the doors. The door opens and a tall gangly man twists and manoeuvres his body through the hatch, hand sliding from the door his body lands in a heap on the platform.

"Jesus mate, you know the rules in this place. You can't spend any more than eight hours plugged into the C-grid without a rest." Below the platform the pepper pot shape of a woman, brown lab coat displaying a badge and sporting faded patches of colour, shakes her head of brown hair. "I've told you a number of times and still you're in there. Listen, I run a respectable place here, not some two bit Manc cyber-shop that will let you die in there. You're too caught up in whatever sordid business you're up to." Twisting a plastic wristband she taps the face like a keyboard.

Slowly the platform moves away, the man's legs dangling over the edge as the door closes with an almost inaudible suck. Lifting his head he rubs the back of his neck. "It hasn't been eight yet?"

The arm slowly trundles across the ceiling, stopping before lowering the platform and depositing the man's limp, sweaty body onto a small plastic mattress in the corner.

The woman follows behind, tapping more buttons on her wrist. "Yes it has, the allotted time you paid for has gone. Go and get some scran and don't come back for at least an hour or you and me will barney. Clear?" The man groans, lifting his head to argue as gravity takes over, his skull crashing back into the cushions. Her eyes drift to Tyler, the scowl disappearing into the smile of an air hostess. "Good evening sir, my name is Sheila and how are you this fine day?" Slowly sidestepping she positions herself between Tyler and the sweat-soaked customer.

Tyler raises an eyebrow. "I'm very well at the moment. Hope I'm not interrupting?"

"Oh no, no sir. May I welcome you to Shelovies and I will be your communicator. Now, how may we be of service?

Rubbing his hands Tyler motions to the wall. "I need a cubicle."

"Yes sir, we can happily arrange this. Do you need any special requirements? Connection plugs, retina scanners, specific security programmes. We have a wide range of additions."

"No, just an interface and normal security functions."

Sheila motions towards the wall of doors. "Well number four, twelve and thirty-seven are available. Number twenty-four has recently become available," her head turns momentarily to the collapsed customer, "and will be ready in about one minute."

"Number four will be fine."

Twisting the metal bracelet again Sheila taps the screen. The door to booth number four, situated at ground level, opens with a hiss, the inside bright with a soft orange luminance. She bows her head. "Climate controls and such essentials are located on the panel next to the screen. I hope you enjoy your time with us. Just enter the required duration and scan your chip on the receiver below the screen."

Nodding, Tyler moves to the door, stepping through. The inside of the booth is a sea of moulded plastic, the seat similar material except for a covering of thick woven padding. Sitting down his eyes shift from corner to corner, scrutinising every inch of the walls and floor. With a deep breath he pulls a screen from a nook in the wall, the keyboard and scanner slowly lowering from the underside as a myriad of colours burst into life on the monitor. He waves the back of his hand over the plate, a momentary collection of chimes ring from the speakers. Rummaging in his bag he pulls out a small wallet-sized box, and removes two small interface plugs from the housing. Plugging one into the underside of the computer he plugs the other into a jack just under his ear. Spasms shoot through his face, his neck twitching as a shiver runs through his entire body. Breathing deeply he closes his eyes as a chorus of beeps drift from the box.

Tyler opens his eyes, vision hazy and static as an old valve television. The snow fades as the sharp edges and corners of the booth come into focus. Opening the door he steps into a field of broken, crumbling buildings, cube-shaped rubble strewn around the base of the walls and doorways. Within his vision the inside edges and corners of the booth linger, like the double exposure of an old paper photograph. Suspended at waist level the ghostly outline of his legs, contours of spectral hands occasionally twitching at chest level. "Ao One. Where are you?"

A voice assaults his ears like the scratching of a chalk

board. Behind a piece of partially collapsed wall a small sphere of light drifts round, coils of glistening tendrils dangle from the base, the whole ball bobbing on small puffs of wind. Sound emanates from within. "Do you possess the box, as requested?"

Tyler smiles, bringing his right hand up and rubbing his fingers together. "Yes, and may I say at considerable expense."

"Your monetary problems are of no concern, your payment remains unchanged."

"This mate is where we disagree, an overhead has arisen that needs to be accounted for."

The sphere drifts closer. "List overhead!"

"Well the damage to my bodyguard's car, considerable in certain areas, means we need another to reach the meeting place."

"Your responsibility as part of our agreement."

"The agreement was for certain expenses, in my opinion this is one of them."

"Your responsibility as part of our agreement."

"Wear and tear on the car yes, this isn't wear and tear. The bloody thing's trashed and unusable, it's not just a quick oil change we're talking here."

"Your responsibility as part of our agreement."

"Without the car we can't meet up and all this is for nothing. Do you want this or not?"

Light flashes within. "Affirmative."

"Good then you had better find the responsibility and get us another car."

"Take the train."

"Listen you stupid fucking Pac-man, this thing is too heavy and dangerous to be carrying around. To top that off, what if we meet trouble? Get us a car or I will find another buyer." Tyler holds his palm out.

136

The sphere drifts backwards a couple of paces, the light inside a dim and distant candle. The sphere's light grows, flickering with an explosion of colours before reducing to a sheet of white. Into his hand a package of bound paper phases into existence. "Documents for a hire car and a gate pass. The meeting will commence in the ruins of the town once known as Ellesmere Port, in the Demon Zone, one hour from now. Failure to meet will result in aggressive liquidation of our agreement. Do you understand?"

"Why the Demon Zone?"

"You have your orders, be there."

"Yeah, whatever. We'll be there." Stepping away he walks back to the booth. Looking back the sphere slowly crumbles into wisps of dust and smoke. Tyler snorts. "See you back in the real world; don't forget your gray overalls."

## Chapter 5

Pulling up in a bus stop Tyler surveys the area, the half broken windows of the cinema in the distance. "Can't see any wildlife out there."

Rang picks up the super soaker from her lap. "The operative word in your sentence is 'see'. I can't see any beasts either, that doesn't mean they're not here. Keep your toy on standby." She opens the door, stepping out into the crisp wet air. "Remember, we've just had a rain storm so most toothy-bite fiends are huddled up in shelters somewhere, trying to stay dry."

Stepping out of the car Tyler moves to the boot, opening the hatch and examining the box. "He should be here soon. Tell you what, I had concerns at that check point, didn't think they were going to let us out."

"The thing is, they're not that bothered what goes out as much as what goes in. First and foremost keep out the fiends, then any contraband, if you're stupid enough to want to go outside the fortification that's your problem. They'll be a lot stricter on the way back. We'll have to dump our weapons and ammo before entering, this thing has no concealed compartments." Rang's eyes snap to the left, the low hum of car engines in the distance.

From the hill crest two black luxury sedans trundle over the roundabout and down the road. One drives past, pulling onto the pavement in front of them, the second parking behind. From each car two men climb out, surveying the area, double barrelled submachine guns in hand. A man steps from the second car, long dark hair blowing in the cold breeze. Crouching back into the car he nods. The fourth passenger door opens, an Armani foot scratching some grip against the overgrown paving slabs. Standing up the tailored form steps onto the pathway, eyes covered with dazzling reflective sunglasses. His flesh is the colour of a corpse, hair slicked back and body encased in a suit of fine light blue cashmere. The glare of wing-tip shoes on his feet and prohibition striped trilby on his head. "You arrived without incident?" His voice skittish like the tone of an automated customer helpline.

Tyler steps from the boot. "Hello Ao, it's nice to see you too. To answer your question, yes. So far, so good."

Ao moves forward a couple of paces, the guard before him stepping into stride. "The merchandise?" The boot of his car opens and the long haired man steps to the back.

Tyler nods. "We have it right here, the question is do you have the money?"

From behind Ao, the long haired man carries a small folding table, setting it in front of the tailored corpse. "Bring the case forward for verification."

Lifting the box from the back Tyler carries it to the table. "I hope you have the key with you or this will be a bit of a waste of time."

Placing his hand in his pocket Ao pulls out a plastic key, a small chip embedded in the handle with stretching metal lines passing through to the tip. Pushing it into the keyhole a trail of lights slowly appear from left to right, then disappear as the box clicks open. Lifting the lid, light dances over Ao's face. Manoeuvring his hands inside he lifts out a basketball sized transparent orb, swirls of colour dancing inside. The orb sits on a connected gold stand of swirling clouds. "Verification complete." He places the orb back in the box. "Payment sent in exactly thirty seconds to the agreed acc..." A distant shot rings out, Ao's forehead explodes in a shower of flesh and shimmering metal. Shot after shot punches holes in three of the guards.

Rang hits the floor, rolling to the side of the car. "Tyler, get down!" Tyler collapses, curling into a ball of leather and cloth. The two remaining guards duck behind the cars, scanning the units of shops either side of the road. Another shot rings out, punching a baseball sized cavity through the front wing of one vehicle, a similar hole appearing in the guard cowering behind it. A second shot pins the final guard against the passenger door, red slowly spreading across the floor. The firing stops, the air still as the depths of the Amazon. Rang kneels behind the car, pulling out her gun. "Stay down for now." Standing she moves towards the table, kneeling down to examine Ao's corpse. "It's dead. The posatrinsic brain unit's smashed, which means the intelligence is dead."

Tyler uncurls to a sitting position. "Is it safe to get up?"

Rang glares at him. "Just do what I say, stay where

you are." She moves to the box, inspecting the outside, then the orb. In the distance the low rumble of cars drifts from behind the units of the outlet village.

Moving to his knees Tyler crawls to the car. "Oh shit, can you hear that?"

Closing the box and pocketing the key Rang kicks Ao's body. "Yes I can."

Reaching the car Tyler starts to rummage in his pocket, fingers touching the car keys. "Quick, we need to get out of here."

Rang walks towards him, reaching into her pocket she pulls out a small, ornately carved metal cylinder. "No we don't." Aiming the muzzle she fires. Four small darts, tethered to the inside of the cylinder embed in the small of his back. Tyler's face contorts, arms and legs twitch and spasm as a small buzzing washes over his body. Still holding the rod Rang moves towards him, pinning his shoulder down and rummaging under his jacket, pulling out his gun. Slipping the weapon into her pocket she disconnects the lines from the rod.

Tyler lays still, body shaking. "What do you mean, you work for me?"

Rang picks up the box. "Technically, I work for DiamondBlue. You hired my services from him, and he wants to thank you for that." She walks back to him. "You see, he knew that any tampering with the box and it would self-destruct. Remember we've dealt with your company before, and we know how you do business." Stopping a few paces away from him the rumble of engines draws closer. "He needed the key and the only way to get it was to wait for you to complete the transaction. Again he thanks you."

Drawing her gun from its holster she pulls back the hammer. "Do you really think I'm stupid enough to believe the bullshit that comes out of your mouth?" She shakes her head. "Now, it is with great sadness that I've got to say our association must end. You can keep the slum lord's money, a gift from me." She levels the gun and smiles. "Let's see if you're allergic to lead." Pulling back on the trigger the gun spits death into Tyler. "I guess you are."

**Damian Steadman**

Damian Steadman was born in Ellesmere Port, Cheshire and attended Manchester Metropolitan University. Writing includes one novel, poems and short stories for publishing consideration. broystheebb@googlemail.com

To my writing club, thanks for your time, my teachers the same. A special thanks to the most important person, my dad, for his infinite patience and love. You guys rock!

## Stranded in Eternity

He revived with a smile on his face. When lay preacher Greg Pacifico opened his eyes he knew that he had died and was finally in heaven. Greg was lying on dewy grass and there were birds singing all around him. The last thing he could remember was driving along a country road at night. It had been winter and he had been on his way back from a church service. He should have been concentrating on the road rather than congratulating himself on the success of his sermon. There was a blur and a moment of confusion as something ran out in front of his car. He had turned the wheel suddenly, skidded on black ice and watched as the trunk of a tree seemed to race towards his windscreen. After this there was just a feverish dream time.

Greg was glad that he had been alone in the car. He had never married and had no close relatives to leave behind. His parents had died when he was young and he had no brothers or sisters. He considered his church friends to be the only family he had. As he looked upwards he could see an angel flying across the blue sky. For a moment he had to check to make sure he was not lying on a fluffy cloud.

Standing up, he brushed the speckles of dew off his clothes and looked around. He was standing in the middle of some kind of a city on a small piece of parkland. He wondered what had happened to the last judgement. This just wasn't scriptural. He thought he had to go before the great white throne and see God before he went to heaven. Why had he gone straight in?

He stood there and had a theological argument inside his head. He reasoned that he had escaped the judgement seat and been allowed into heaven because he was a

Christian and was saved. He remembered his many doubts and reconsidered. Perhaps he was in that period where he would soon approach the place where the rewards are handed out to God's faithful servants. No, if that was the case he would have been led to some kind of throne room. In the end he half-decided that he must be in paradise, the place saved souls went *before* the judgement. That would explain things.

Then the full enormity of what had happened hit him. This was it, this was what he had been waiting and longing for all his earthly life. Tears of joy filled his eyes and Greg fell to his knees and lifted his hands into the air. "Hallelujah!" he shouted, knowing for once that God could hear him. Tears filled his eyes. At last he knew it was all real, at last he knew he had chosen the right path. He had finally reached his promised land.

Greg looked down at his clothes. He was dressed in a white shirt, blue jeans and a red jacket. After a few more tears he finally looked around properly. Some of his surroundings looked virtually impossible. The height of the buildings grew taller the closer they got to the city centre. Far above, he could see a skyscraper which stretched so far into the sky that he almost couldn't see the top. He knew his Bible well, and he knew that heaven's first city was supposed to be as tall as it was wide. Was this what the scripture meant? He could hear music coming from the distance. He stopped and listened, then smiled as he recognised the tune. It was William Blake's hymn 'Jerusalem', one of his favourites.

The pavement near the grass lawn where he had been lying was so shiny that he could see his face in it. The streets were made from a smooth, reflective gold. In places the gold was cobbled and each cobble was like a huge golden nugget.

When he did go and look at himself in one of these golden mirrors he got his first shock. He was many years *older* than he had ever been. His last memories were of being a healthy 29 year-old. And here he was looking about 59! His hair was grey and he could clearly see wrinkles around his eyes and mouth. His forehead was now furrowed with lines.

He began to walk through the city and soon came to a river and more parkland. There were people all around. Many of the people were in deep conversation. One man pointed into the sky. When Greg followed the man's gaze he realized that he was pointing at one of the angels. There were a lot of angels. Some of the people were being carried. They buzzed through the sky like daddy-long-legs' – all legs and wings. Greg couldn't see any cars or other kinds of transport.

"The perfect answer to pollution!" he exclaimed aloud.

He had always hoped that in heaven he'd be able to fly and would have a whole new kind of body. And this was his second shock. His body still ached. He knew *that* shouldn't be happening. Wasn't pain supposed to be outlawed? In fact, he *felt* the 30 years older that he looked.

Greg carried on walking. Despite his initial disappointments he had to admit that he was now in a place very different to the world he had left. He began to walk down one of the gold streets which followed the river and he could see trees lining the riverbanks. The trees were unlike any he had ever seen before. The leaves on these trees were transparent, like see-through sweet wrappers. They were shaped like diamonds and the light shone through them and made them shine so brilliantly that he wondered if those leaves were made of thin crystal or perhaps even pieces of real diamond. If this was heaven, surely *anything* could be real.

Ahead of him he could see a group of about a hundred people who seemed to be listening intently to someone in the centre of their group. There was a woman walking nearby. Suddenly she quickened her walking pace and began to run towards this group. She was clearly excited. When Greg arrived he was able to get through to a good viewing spot.

There was a man sitting on a rock near the river bank. Unlike the rest of the people, who were dressed in similar clothes to Greg (as if it was some kind of uniform), the man on the rock was dressed in a grey and brown robe, like something out of a history book. He looked stocky and had a black beard, moustache and dark complexion. Greg had approached just as the man finished telling a story to the large group.

"…because when we travelled together he would always get up so early."

The man had a deep, earthy voice.

"Then he would disappear somewhere and come back smiling like he had just had some sort of adventure. Sometimes, we stayed in other people's houses and they knew he had sneaked out during the night. So thank you for listening. But before I finish let me tell you one last memory, and you can tell the person in question that I, Simon Peter told you this. We did so much walking and I remember one day, near the start, Thomas fainted from heat exhaustion, somewhere in Galilee. We didn't know what to do. But when the Lord appeared he just placed his hand on Thomas's head and he came to. Can you imagine that? The great disciple Thomas fainting? Thomas would kill me if he heard me tell you this story… but you can ask him about it, you will find him near the West of the city."

Simon Peter then raised both his arms into the air and shouted, "Long live the revival!"

The people clapped and most began to disperse. Some of them stayed behind, wanting to shake Simon Peter's hand. Others wanted to hug him. All the time Greg stood watching this man who he had read about so often. He could hear the river behind him. It was hypnotic. Simon Peter looked across to the river and seemed to be watching the running water. Greg turned and looked as well. There were fish in it, fish so huge and colourful that he really couldn't name them. There were bathers further along, some of them wading, others swimming in the clear water. Suddenly, he watched as one of the fish leapt out of the water, and stretched out white wings which were shaped like a butterfly's. Then it just flew up, from the water into the sky and out into the distance.

Simon Peter also watched it go and said, "I'm going to catch one of them."

"He always says that," commented one of the bystanders.

Greg decided he would ask Simon Peter to tell him exactly what was happening. If he was in heaven, what was he supposed to do? This was all so... sudden. Would he be able to see his parents? He hadn't seen them in years and even the grief of losing them so young had seemed to heal with time.

He walked up to the disciple, who was still sitting on the rock watching the river. There were a few people still milling around and Greg decided he would go up and shake Simon Peter's hand and then get into a conversation. When he did, he noticed that his hand was cold and his grip was strong.

"I've always wanted to meet you..." blurted Greg, "...I... I'm new here and, I was wondering if you could help me with a few things... questions really."

The disciple smiled.

That was when Greg noticed Simon Peter's eyes. Close up his irises were jet black. It gave the impression that his pupils were completely dilated, but it wasn't that, it was just that he had black coloured irises.

Suddenly one of the angels approached the few people left around Simon Peter and began to motion for them to move on. Greg was caught up with them and involuntarily led away. When the angel had stopped pushing them around Greg decided that it would be able to tell him exactly what was happening and what he should do as a newcomer. The angels were all tall, and they all looked the same. Some had different coloured hair. But they all looked alike, all of them with wings like birds, exactly the same facial features and skin which looked more like copper metal than flesh. It was hard to tell whether they were male or female, they were hermaphrodites. But like Simon Peter, they too had strange jet black eyes.

"I need some help to get my bearings." It was all Greg could think of to say.

The angel was completely silent.

"This is great… amazing really. But I have some questions."

The angel said nothing and looked blank.

"Did I die? I remember crashing, but not much else? Are my parents here?"

Still the angel just stood there, as if it was deaf and dumb.

Completely at a loss, Greg blurted out, "Do I have a mansion?"

The angel spoke in a monotone, almost lifeless voice.

"Where would you like to go?"

Greg looked around at all the people packing the city streets.

147

"Home, I want to go home," replied Greg.

"You are home," said the angel. "Where would you like to go?"

"Somewhere peaceful then," said Greg finally, shaking his head in confusion, "out of this place, somewhere I can think."

With these words, the angel took his hand and grabbed him around the waist. He felt himself being tugged into the air. Soon he was lifted high above the city.

It was like flying in a helicopter. Some of the buildings now looked like dominoes below, while the taller ones still stood much higher. And there was always the glow from the gold on the streets, as if the city itself was a jewel, with a sparkling river, like a fault, streaking its way through it all.

"I suppose you've got to create something which will appeal to the majority without alienating individuals and their own personal preferences!" he shouted.

But the angel couldn't hear him and the sound of the wind and the angel's wings stopped them from communicating. They flew out past the city wall. The river ran out through a tunnel in the side of one of the walls into sudden countryside. There were no suburbs, no greenbelt, just hills and woods. From urban to rural in a moment. Then there were the valleys and gorges which looked like something straight from a picture postcard. There were clear lakes. One or two of the lakes looked different. One of them looked like it was filled with something golden brown in colour. Another one looked like it was full of milk. "A land flowing with milk and honey," laughed Greg into the wind.

For a while a flock of geese flew in an arrow formation behind them. The sun reflected with an orange glow on the bird's underbellies. Eventually they left the geese and flew low.

Finally, the angel landed near a waterfall in an isolated valley.

"This is called 'Morning Star Falls'," said the angel, "it is a peaceful place. I shall come to collect you in four hours."

The angel then raised its arms like Simon Peter had done and intoned, "Long live the revival."

"Likewise," replied Greg, half-heartedly lifting one of his aching arms.

The flight had been uncomfortable and Greg was still wondering why he had aches and pains. But before he could ask, the angel had flown away.

Despite the loud crashing noise of the waterfall, Greg appreciated the peace. The waterfall parted in many places, so that the whole effect was like a tree turned upside down. A cool drizzle sprayed his face. Greg felt sure that he could hear music playing in the distance. There were caves in the cliff face over which the water plunged.

There were birds and a couple of rabbits near the trees which surrounded the waterfall. But some of the vegetation was more like coral on land than the usual plant life. Greg felt the same way he had felt when he had visited Disneyland when he was a boy. It was the last holiday he had had with his parents.

A vine covered part of the cliff and it looked almost like frost. He went up to it and touched it. It felt like glass. Some of the more ordinary looking trees had jewels embedded into their bark. He moved on, closer to the bank of the waterfall.

There was a solitary flower growing near the water. It was a blue rose. Greg leaned forward to smell it but could smell nothing from the flower. However, when he leaned in closer he realized that the music was coming out of the rose. It was an eerie sound, like that which a flute can make.

Further ahead, Greg found a single tree with golden leaves. Or, more accurately, the leaves themselves were made out of strips of gold. The trunk of the tree was an ordinary brown and was hollow and he could see that there was a space large enough for someone to stand inside. He reached up and snapped one of the solid gold leaves from a low branch. The leaf looked real enough, it was hard and thin. He wondered if it was really gold and placed it in his trouser pocket. Then he wondered if he was stealing. There was pain, so what if it was possible to sin here too? Surely not. But why had the thought come? Still, he decided that there should, at least, be freedom in Heaven, so he decided to keep the leaf. He then stepped into the hollow tree.

He sat down and leaned against the inside trunk. So much had happened and he felt that he needed to think. When Greg wrote his sermons he always used to sit down, close his eyes and let the ideas come. As he did this he was calmed by the sound of the waterfall, the birds and the strange song of the blue rose. Before he knew it he was asleep.

It was night time in the dream. He felt vulnerable. He was sitting at the base of a high, rocky hill. The moon was full and there was water trickling nearby. Something made him look up to the top of the hill. There was a black shadow up there, rising into the sky, a huge dark silhouette perched on a rocky outcrop near the top. He tried to make out what the thing was. Suddenly the silhouette grew in size and he realized with a jolt that it was extending thick wings. And the wings shone dazzling colours, as if they were made out of stained glass. Moonlight was shining through them. Greg felt afraid. He knew that the thing was looking straight at him. He got to his feet and prepared to run away but found himself glued to the spot. Then the dark thing began to move down the hillside, its huge muscular legs and clawed feet ripping through the vegetation. It got closer and closer and he felt fear rising into his throat. His throat felt like it was sealed with a stone so that he couldn't even scream. In a matter of seconds the creature was upon him. He watched as one of its giant horned heads towered above him before the bite. The last thing he saw were its steely, black eyes looking on him only with hatred.

He woke abruptly, aching from lying foetus-like on the hard ground inside the tree. Slowly he got to his feet and left the tree. With a shock he realized that it was approaching dusk. The sky was much darker now. Greg remembered when a fellow churchgoer had once objected to there not being any night in the afterlife and Greg had told that person that he was sure God would provide the things they liked about the night, carelessly suggesting that there would be huge planetariums for people who felt nostalgic for night-time. And now here was the sun, clearly setting in the distance. Had he taken scripture too literally all his life?

Walking back towards the waterfall he noticed something half-hidden in the vegetation near the water. It was a dead rabbit covered in flies.

"Have you enjoyed your time here at Morning Star Falls?" The angel had arrived silently. Greg was not even sure if it was the same angel. They all looked alike.

"It has been surreal," he said bitterly.

The angel extended a hand. "Come. I can take you

back to the city now if you wish."

"Perhaps later, I have a few pressing questions which I must have answered," said Greg firmly.

"Why do I look so much older here?"

The angel nodded and unfolded its wings but said nothing.

"What is this place, really?"

The angel replied, "You are in the new Jerusalem. You are in the heavenly country."

"Then why can I still feel pain?" he asked.

But the angel kept its nonchalant expression and was silent again.

"My parents," said Greg, "are they here?"

More silence.

"And that," he turned and pointed towards the half-decayed rabbit. "There is supposed to be no death here. Why is it dead then?"

Greg felt sure that the angel sneered as it spoke, "Long live the revival. Where would you like to go?"

Finding all the courage that he had within him he formed the words which had been on his mind since he had woken up.

Greg coughed and tried to look authoritative. "I want to be taken to God."

With that the angel took Greg's hand and waist as it had done before and they flew away from Morning Star Falls.

One thing he felt sure of, as they flew across the beautiful countryside. Wherever he was there doubt, death and darkness. What if he was separated from God forever and he was really in... the other place, and all this was part of the cruel joke. What if God turned out to be Lucifer? As they flew back to the walls of the city and landed just outside, Greg began to feel a little afraid. Perhaps he had just expected too much. Was he being a little hasty asking to see God himself?

The city still shone in the dusk light. It was filled with pinprick lights which looked very much like electric lamps. They landed and the angel released him. In front of them both stood a massive pearly gate with fire lit torches each side. The gate was huge and solid and looked like it was either made out of a giant pearl or covered in a mother of pearl veneer.

"That must have come from a big oyster," commented Greg in wonder.

"If I showed you how it was made you wouldn't believe it."

The new voice startled Greg and made him turn. Next to the angel stood young blonde-haired man dressed in a white suit.

"We wondered how you would react to all this. I hope I can answer some of your questions. Let's go somewhere where we can talk properly."

The blonde haired man led him through a smaller entrance near the pearl gate. They walked along the inside of the city wall. They came to a doorway, guarded by two angels and were allowed to walk straight in.

Soon they were standing inside the city wall itself. They had entered a large room filled with computers, machinery and workers meandering to and fro.

"Long live the revival," said one of the workers to the blonde man.

"Long live the revival," he replied.

Greg was led to a back room where a huge cinema screen dominated one of the walls. He was invited to take a seat in front of the screen and the man introduced himself.

"My name is Liam Parker and I am the current leader of the revivalist movement here in Britain. I am privileged to meet with you; I've heard that you were among the pioneers of the great revival. The Christian National Unionist party is entering an historic and unprecedented eighth term..."

Greg interrupted, "I don't know what you're talking about... isn't this supposed to be heaven?"

"You did believe it then!" Liam suddenly looked happy. "The cabinet will be pleased about that. I see that you don't remember much, but it's not surprising following your car crash and the subsequent events. You have been in a coma for 30 years. When we realized you were going to come out of it we took you from the hospital and left you in the city where we could watch your reaction. You have to understand that you represented an opportunity too good to miss. You are a pioneer of the revival, and you have never seen the mammoth changes which have taken place in the last thirty years."

Greg was too stunned to say anything. How could this be the future? If he was still in Britain, why were there angels? And what about all the things he had seen? He forced himself to keep listening.

"Perhaps if I show you something it will make things a bit clearer for you."

Suddenly the light faded and the screen burst into life. The face of the man who called himself Liam Parker appeared there. On the film he said: "As you all know the electorate have been complaining about a sense of discontinuity and a lack of national identity. The lack of national identity has partly arisen through our building over many of Britain's famous landmarks, St Paul's, Westminster, Stonehenge etc. It is also due to an ignorance of our national destiny. There is currently a great disunity in the country. The people are at a place where they feel unable to define themselves. We need a common enemy. We have already shared and fulfilled much of our original vision. Now that we have fulfilled our electoral promises and built, in effect, a heaven on earth, it seems important to take stock and remind the people of what we have already accomplished.

"Thirty years ago we experienced the biggest revival the country has ever had. A revival which gave birth to the CNU and marked the beginning of our work to create a sustainable paradise here in Britain. As a result of the success of that vision and the current crisis in identity we have made a new party political broadcast which will be shown throughout the country. We thought it only fair to show the grass root workers, our precious party members who, in effect, are running this country, a first showing of the broadcast. So please keep watching."

The film then showed Britain as Greg had known it. Except everything was shown in black and white. He could see London's streets, the Houses of Parliament and people walking through city streets on their way to work. He could see trains and buses and houses with people watching their TV. He noted that the TV screen one family was watching was showing a Conservative Party political broadcast. Then music began in the background. It was Blake's 'Jerusalem' again.

Colour filled the screen. A woman's voice was now speaking over images of marches and mass celebrations in the streets.

"Since the revival began we have been searching," said the voice, "searching for God and searching for a better world. The Christian National Unionists were voted in on the heels of the revival. We promised to change things. We promised to take Britain into a new era." There

155

were images of building and destruction. London was levelled to the ground and new buildings were put in the place of the old ones. Then one of the angels filled the screen. "Through technological advances, a gift from God to be used for his glory, we were able to make the angels. We promised you things would be different and that we would build a modern Constantinople. 'The earth is the Lord's and all who live in it'. We promised you a model country, a beacon of light to the rest of the world, based on the Biblical principles of heaven with democracy at its best. A vision for the people. A promised land. A new Jerusalem." The angel disappeared to show the city Greg had been to. "We got our best architects, thinkers, designers, artists and great minds to work on making the vision a reality. We kept the best of the old and added the new. What we couldn't do for real," here there was a picture of a gold street; "We made to look real. Or so real that it wouldn't matter.

We live in a new world, a world which has been swept by the spirit of Christian revival. The CNU has promised that our mission will continue in order to fulfil the whole vision." A group of men appeared on the screen and Greg recognised the man he had seen at the riverside, who he had thought was Simon Peter, standing among them.

"We created working and historically accurate representations of the apostles. Now..." Suddenly the scene changed dramatically. On the screen was something hideous which Greg recognized. A monstrous black dragon swooped down above the city. Greg guessed that it was computer generated, but it was still terrifying. It had seven heads which instead of spewing flames were jetting out ice over the people below. Its wings were black, like a bat's wings, but multi-coloured, the same stained-glass as in his nightmare. Each head was filled with ferocious teeth and had a bony mantle shaped like a horny crown. The dragon swooped across the city, almost crashing into the giant skyscraper, but flying around it.

"...we are facing an enemy so dangerous that we all must unite against it. Evil is returning. All it takes is for good men and women to do nothing for evil to triumph." The dragon disappeared and the picture changed to a view of a massive throne room he had never seen. "And so now we are preparing the earth. But one day, the culmination of all history will take place. One day our saviour will rule with us. And..." The camera began to zoom in on a white ivory throne. "...soon he will be here with us. Vote CNU. Long live the revival."

After this the screen went blank. Liam grinned, turned to Greg and said, "You won't remember the revival. I was a boy when it happened. It swept through the world like a wave. Like a fire. It was as unstoppable as it was unexpected. A landslide victory for the revivalists. And it marked a twist in our national narrative. But what do you think of all this, Greg?"

Greg had been listening up until then, with an array of emotions surfacing within him as he had watched the screen and listened to Liam's explanation of his situation. Most of all Greg felt he had been tricked. He felt as if he was part of a huge practical joke which everyone except him was in on.

He said, "I hoped I was on the other side of eternity. Now you say I'm not and I don't know what to think. I want to go home. This isn't what I prayed for."

Liam's brow furrowed.

"You mean you don't believe in democracy either? The majority are believers now, so why shouldn't we want to change things? We've turned things around. Democracy

157

is no longer like two wolves and a sheep voting on what they are going to have for lunch – it is the sheep who get the vote now. Ironic.

"This isn't the tyranny of the majority you know? People are still free to believe what they like... within the limits of the new laws. I'd have thought you would be pleased to see the fruits of your prayers. Others are."

"This is not what I prayed for," repeated Greg, "I was always happy to see Christians involved in politics. But this façade you have created is nothing short of idolatrous. What will you make next? Christ himself?"

Liam turned his back on Greg.

"We thought we'd leave him out of this."

"That's obvious," said Greg sarcastically.

Liam shrugged. "There have been calls for creating a working model of Christ, to place him within the city, but it is something the party continues to resist. What we have looked into is the call for a common enemy for us all to stand up against."

"You really don't get it, do you? You may have turned everything upside down, but some things were already the right way up. Why did you need to make Britain look like heaven? Why did you demolish the country? Why not just live differently and love each other. Why did you have to have everything so... so... man-made?"

Liam smiled then.

"Greg, we have created a society better than the one you remember. The crime figures are almost nil and many of the problems you will have lived with all your life no longer exist now. Drug use is almost non-existent; the God-shaped hole in the hearts of the people has been filled. Hurting people have invited Jesus into what was left of their hearts. The people were sick, they were broken, now they are mended, healed. What is so wrong with what we have done? Shouldn't heaven be a democracy too?

We're not hedonists, but we know that people are happier these days. And they really do believe you know? Christianity went mainstream. If there were dinosaurs who couldn't accept that happening it was them that needed to change and not us. I would have thought you would have been pleased. Millions were *saved* Greg. I understand that this is a big thing for you. But don't be so eager to condemn the changes, because we did it for people like you."

Greg shook his head.

"What is going to happen to me?"

"We will provide for you. The love which you spoke of is here too. Despite your doubts we will make sure that you are taken care of. There is plenty of time."

"But not eternity," said Greg with tears coming to his eyes.

Liam stood up and walked to the door.

"You need to be alone for a while," he said and left.

"It's a sick joke," said Greg when he had finished crying. There was no one in the room. But Greg didn't care. "This isn't Britain, this isn't heaven, it's the other place. I'm surrounded by devils that don't care. I did die. And this is the devil's joke on me."

That was when he spotted the air vent at the base of one of the walls. He stood up and walked across to it, crouching down. The ventilation system was large enough to crawl inside if he could remove the cover. The cover was a grill with large screws holding it in place. Greg took the gold leaf from the tree at Morning Star Falls out of his pocket and slotted its thin edge into the groove of one of the screws. It turned. Then he began to work at each screw, eventually opening up the grill. Once he had climbed in, there was just enough space to turn and pull the grill into place once again. Then he began to crawl.

The ventilation duct continued further than he thought it would, branching off in places. Greg took one of the turnings and suddenly the light from the room was gone. In front of him was just darkness. He shuffled along on his belly with his arms in front of him, feeling the smooth walls. He was now travelling along a fairly straight gradient downwards. It was impossible to see anything; all he could hear was a slow humming noise. There was no way he could turn around now.

He didn't know how long he continued like this, crawling along the dark ventilation shaft. It continued to lead downwards. He was moving slowly, he didn't want to fall down some hidden hole. But he made good progress.

More than once he came to a turning, but he determined that he would try to find a way out and followed a way which he thought would lead him towards the outside world. He desperately wanted the tunnel to begin to head upwards again, but he was just climbing deeper and deeper into the ground and the shaft just seemed to continue downwards. Strangely the air was getting warmer the further he went along. Eventually, the tunnel became so narrow that it seemed like there was no way to continue. Except he could see a small glow from a yellow light coming from somewhere ahead. Soon he could hear the murmur of raised voices mixing with a low groaning. He came to another turning and suddenly there was a fiery light in front of him.

He had to forcibly push away the grill. It clattered to the floor, but the sound was drowned out by groaning of what he realized was machinery. He climbed out into a huge room, hidden behind a large computer console. The fiery light was coming from a set of computer screens. At first the light from the screens was too bright for his eyes.

He was in a vast underground cavern which was filled with people. There was machinery everywhere and the people were dressed in white lab-coats and hard-hats with torches on them. At the far end of the cavern there was something which looked like a huge statue covered by a cloth, like a piece of art waiting to be unveiled. He stopped, looking at the way he had come in. From his position crouched behind the console he could safely look at all the activity so that he would not be seen, providing none of the people looked his way from their clipboards and computers.

It took him a while before he realized that the screens were showing scenes from a torch lit 'heaven'. One of them showed part of the city with people walking around and angels flying through the air. There were so many scenes that the whole display made him feel dizzy and he had to steady himself.

He waited there for what seemed like hours, not daring to move, too afraid to show himself and too tired to go back the way he had come. Suddenly there was an announcement which filled the cavern: "Party workers, please come to the prayer hall for your morning quiet time."

The workers began to leave the cavern. Soon there was no-one left. Greg waited until he was sure that no-one was coming back in and stood up.

He walked across to the far side of the cavern to the covered artwork he had noticed which filled part of the hall. There were ropes holding the covering and Greg began to untie them. He worked at each rope, loosening the knots and moving on to the next rope when he had finished. Finally there was one rope to untie left. As soon as he loosened it, the cover fell away.

Greg's mouth fell open.

161

In front of him was the multi-headed dragon he had seen in the CNU's party political broadcast and in his dream. It was motionless, but still terrifying. Its eyes were black, like all the robots. Its wings were as beautiful as Lucifer before his fall. Greg turned, grabbed a metal chair and swung it down on the nearest head. There were sparks as Greg dealt what would have been a mortal wound if the dragon was real. Instead he left one of the heads hanging loose with wires exposed.

That was when Liam Parker entered the cavern.

He walked up to Greg and the dragon. "If you feel so antagonistic towards us, then join us, help us to change, help us to remember what the revival was all about. Don't just hit out at us. Help us to change, to keep moving... like you always did. Remember Greg, things are better now. We've made things better."

For a brief moment Greg thought back to his parents and thought of the joy he had felt in Disneyland with them. It had all been man-made, but there had been a magic to it as well. It was a magic which transcended everything made by humans. And it whispered healing words.

He turned and faced Liam and ran his hand through his own greying hair. The words which came out of his mouth surprised even him. "Well, for a start," he said pointing to the dragon, "*that* is a really bad idea."

**Nick White**

Nick White is a writer living in Staffordshire. His website is www.nickwhitewriting.com. This story is dedicated to his wife, Jen.

# The Outliners

```
Destination: Earth
Human subjects: Harry, Eloise, Eleanor
and Eleni Stone
Creative Gift: Artist
Mission: Identify, study and implement
the fecundity gene
Projected Outcome: 100% expected suc-
cess
```

The alien looked at the words suspended symmetrically in front of him. The need for screens had disappeared thousands of years ago.

It studied the four names and immediately four images formed next to the words.

Interesting, was its first thought. Its second thought was how easy this mission was going to be.

"Harry, can you make sure the girls manage to put something in their mouths this morning? I'm going up stairs to get a shower." His mum didn't wait for a reply because it wasn't a question. Harry could already hear the electric shower revving up.

He put his book down next to the cereal bowl and glanced across at his three sisters, lined up neatly on the other side of the table. They really were identical, he couldn't tell them apart. Eloise, Eleanor and Eleni. Wasn't it bad enough being identical? Why did his parents have to be alliterative in the naming of their belated offspring too?

All three watched him. As though even their eyes functioned in unison.

Harry practically threw his bowl into the sink. He heard a faint crack as it hit the bottom. He then went to tend to his triplet, fifteen-month-old sisters. It was true; most of their food lay strewn across the tables of their high chairs. Eloise, Eleanor and Eleni looked up expectantly towards their brother and six eyes lit up simultaneously. Harry smiled at them and screwed his face up. All three began to giggle. *They were cute,* but he was still annoyed that his mother thought it was okay to land him the job of over-seeing his sisters' breakfast routine.

He bent down to clear up some of the cereal that had been thrown on the floor. As he straightened, he smelt the obvious odour of, he thought, Eloise's soiled nappy.

"God, that really is foul." He picked her out of the high chair, ready to march upstairs with the toddler held as far away as possible from his nose.

"Where you going, Harry? She hasn't finished her breakfast yet."

His mum was standing in the doorway of the kitchen, a towel wrapped firmly around her head. He handed the child over to her.

"Can't do nappies, Mum..."

"Well, you should learn." She looked at him, unravelling her towel turban at the same time. "How much are your driving lessons...? Harry knew what she was alluding to. He didn't answer. "Forty pounds a throw – not much to ask as reciprocal payment, to make sure your sisters don't starve and a few nappy changes...?

"Come on, Mum – they're not mine. You had them. It's not fair."

"Life's not fair, Harry." She walked towards the table and picked up his half-read book; Eloise sat grumpily on her hip. "What's this? This *is not* your English home-work." She read the title out loud. "*Creating Modern Art.*" She looked at her son. "Harry, I know you want to be an artist – and that's great – but your English grades are awful... I know, I know, it isn't all about academia, it's about being creative and doing what you want to do, it's all about ideas, and Harry, your artwork is wonderful. But. The bottom line is, you need to pass your A levels.' Gently she placed book back down. "It's important."

"Give it a break – I get the picture." He took his sister from his mother's hip. Eloise began to whimper. "I'll go and change her nappy." Harry disappeared up the stairs; his heavy footsteps made the staircase shudder under the strain.

Harry did change his sister's nappy and hummed quietly to her as he did so. And he did feel marginally guilty about what he had said to his mum regarding the birth of his triplet sisters. Harry had been as ecstatic as his mum and dad when they were born. But he didn't feel too guilty, for Christ sakes he was seventeen and didn't have time for babies. Even if they were his sisters.

After he'd finished the nappy change, Harry lay on the bed with Eloise happily lying on his stomach.

The bus stopped outside the sixth form college. It took Harry zero seconds to decide he wasn't going in today. He had made up his mind long before the bus stopped. He'd decided while he was changing Eloise's nappy. His mother was taking the girls to his gran's and probably wouldn't be back until late evening. His dad was out of the country, in Houston, the U S of A, on business for over a month. The house would be empty.

Harry stayed on the bus for the round trip home. As he was about to jump off he caught the driver turning his head.

Harry looked him straight in the face. "Revision at home."

"Yeah, right," the driver replied.

165

He hoped the bus driver didn't know either of his parents.

Harry jogged to his front door and rang the bell, just in case. No one was home.

The kitchen was tidy apart from the triplet's dirty plastic dishes and beakers in the sink. Quickly Harry washed them up and wiped down the work surfaces.

Harry's book still lay on the table. He picked it up and went through the lounge towards the patio doors. He opened them and a weird mid-February warmth enveloped him. He loved to sit on the raised patio to read, sketch a few ideas, and generally be *creative*. It was his favourite spot, especially when the house was quiet.

The view of the long, narrow garden was uninterrupted. He always found the scene and the quietness inspiring; and he certainly needed some inspiration – from somewhere. The rejection letters from the art magazines were building up.

Harry knew he wasn't quite good enough. The editors and art gallery managers who bothered to scrawl something at the bottom of the impersonal, standard letters of rejection told him so. But he was always dreaming of success; he couldn't stop himself. He was absorbed in the book when he heard a distinct noise, made from the movement of joined timber, and not a sound made from the weight of a squirrel – or cat. Something much heavier. He squinted towards the bottom of the garden; the tree house his dad had built for him glinted in the sunshine. His dad had made an excellent job of it – a carpenter's masterpiece. However, it wasn't the tree house that caught Harry's attention but the massive tree it sat in.

Harry scrutinised the thick branches. He could see something; maybe it was a pigeon, or a cat, but as soon as his attention moved towards the tree whatever had been moving, stopped. He picked up his book and carried on reading.

There it was again, a noise, and more than just a rustle of branches. Harry could just about pick up a high-pitched sound.

The ginger tom who lived next door, but who saw their garden as his territory, had been sitting contently very near to Harry. Their garden attracted all the cats in the neighbourhood. It bothered his mum, but Harry loved cats. As the noise disappeared from his hearing range the cat jumped up so vehemently, he landed on his back. The ginger lay there, immobilized, his eyes staring.

"What's up, mate – you're a cat, you're not supposed to do that."

The ginger stared at him. His eyes were not dazed. They were glazed. It took Harry a few minutes to realise; the majestic ginger was dead. He stroked the cat's stomach gently and felt the sting of tears in his eyes.

There was a definite movement in the tree. His ears hurt. Harry left the prostrate cat and began to jog down the damp grass of the long garden, maintaining eye contact with the figure he was certain he could see in the tree. Whatever it was, it wasn't human. He could see the outline. It seemed to be part of the green branches. It was camouflaged but every so often Harry saw the outline move. It darted, and appeared to be able to move from one level of the tree to another as if there was more than one person, or thing, up there. His heart was pumping at a speed he normally only managed when he was sprinting the two hundred metres.

He shouted up to the tree, "What is it? What are you?"

There was silence. Harry's head still hurt. More than a headache; it felt like something was inside his brain, inside his skull. What the hell was going on? He stood for minutes, waiting. Waiting for what, he had no idea. Of course there was nothing in the tree. He was going mad; his imagination was taking over. His mum was forever telling him about his overactive and fertile imagination. He needed to drink some water. Rehydrate. God, he sounded like his mother. He sighed and began to turn around.

And then stopped.

From the corner of his eye he saw the outline. It was as though the branches of the tree were alive. He bent forwards, holding his head in both hands – he couldn't remember a headache like this. There was no room for his own thoughts, no space for his brain. And then Harry felt a vague, insidious detachment, as if he was leaving himself, and happy to do so. His usually clear thoughts began slowly to dissipate.

The alien was now inside the tree house. Watching. It would leave nothing behind when it vacated the lovingly built wooden house – only a faint aroma of rotting leaves. And a slight feeling of unearthliness.

Harry lay on the sofa, his drawing pad nestled snugly on his lap. He was concentrating. The idea formed easily in his head. The lines flowed; the picture emerged smoothly onto the page, the proportions of the imagined objects were perfect. He made his way upstairs to find a large envelope. Patiently he placed the work inside, and sealed it with odd tasting saliva. He was putting it neatly on his desk when the phone rang.

"Hi Mother," he said into the phone while lovingly rubbing the edge of the envelope.

"Hi Harry – how did you know it was me?"

"Wild guess."

"Honey, we're going to stay at Gran's tonight. There's lasagne in the fridge – you'll be okay won't you?… or do you want us to come home?"

"Fine."

"Harry, are you okay? Are you…"

"I've done my homework. Have a nice time at Gran's."

"…maybe we should come home…"

"The girls are already in bed, asleep, Mother – why come home?"

"How did you know they were already in bed? And what's with the 'Mother' Harry?"

"See you tomorrow… Mother." Harry placed the phone gently down into its cradle. There was no possibility his mother would be coming home tonight. He knew because the thing from the tree house was telling him so.

Harry went into the kitchen and found the lasagne. He put it in the microwave. The noise from the small oven dug deep into his head. He couldn't bear it. Switching it off he took the lasagne out. After one mouthful of the cold meat pasta Harry decided he didn't need food.

He sauntered into the lounge and opened the patio doors. He looked down towards the tree house. It looked empty but he knew it wasn't. He looked sideways towards the edge of the paving; the cat still lay where it had fallen. Harry knew it wouldn't be there by morning – the foxes would have had it by then.

It was only eight o clock but he decided to go to bed. He was tired. He would post the picture to the publisher in the morning. There was no rush; this time he knew it was a winner.

Harry went upstairs. He didn't take his clothes off and he didn't brush his teeth. He got straight into bed and fell asleep. It was important that he did, because in his dreams he would find a little more, if not the real reason why the Outliner was living in his head, but at least he would find out where the Outliner came from.

Harry wasn't dreaming. His body lifted effortlessly from his bed and moved precisely, head first, through the big dormer window. Was he awake? He thought so. He floated easily down the garden; it took only a few seconds for his body to reach the tree house. He was too wide to fit through the tree house window. Harry watched, detached, as his body narrowed so that it was able to move through the narrow gap.

This wasn't the tree house of his childhood. His childhood was very long gone. This was a dark and cavernous place. Only dots of blue light illuminated it. It felt like there were aliens everywhere, hiding in places he could never hope to see. There was though, only one alien in what he knew was a spaceship.

Harry's mind was taken up with wanting to know more; it wanted to create superb, unique works of art, understand the creative process which would catapult him into a world to which he so wanted to belong. There was some sort of deal going on. A deal with a thing not of this earth; but a thing which, very much wanted to be.

Harry looked own at his body. It had disappeared.

It was now just an Outline. An Outline not of his body, but of a form that would be now existing tens of millions of miles away, in a galaxy that even Harry's lateral and creative mind was unable to comprehend, let alone make up and draw. But his newer, other mind could; and why he was certain of his creative success. Harry was aware the Outliners were more advanced than the humans they wished to study; that there was something they desperately wanted. Deep in what he had thought were dreams the Outliner promised it to him: that if he opened his mind, easily and of his own volition, Harry could have everything he wished for. No one would be able to resist his art. It would be so excellent, so authentic. His art would blow the art world's collective mind. And if they had any mind

170

at all to reject his work, Harry knew they would not and could not. Such was the power of the Outliner in his immense, camouflaged spaceship.

It was important to the alien that Harry spent as much time at as possible at his home. The nearer the human subject was to the tree house, the more it would be able to access the last vestiges of his mind. This infiltration was proving more difficult than the alien had anticipated; a vast amount of telepathic conversation was being exchanged between the inhabitant of the spaceship and its Superior in a far off Galaxy.

The human race was in its infancy; their minds and brains should have been easy to conquer. But the alien had been surprised at the resilience. There seemed to be something in the human brain which they had a problem controlling. For all their technology and understanding of everything that stretched from Earth to their own galaxy, they were unable to conquer some small thing in the human organ. That thing was intangible. Not organic. It was unique to the human race. A religious human would call it the soul; a human biologist would perhaps call it a certain gene, a miniscule part of the DNA, which had yet to be categorised. Whatever it was; it was impossible for the aliens to decipher. If they had any emotions at all, they would have become angry as their ultimate plan and conclusion was slowed. But it would be fair to say that any emotion the aliens had once had, perhaps many millions of years ago, had been effectively eradicated. That was why they had been so successful in their longevity.

Harry's mother and triplet sisters arrived home the next day, mid-afternoon. He was sitting at his desk drawing and painting. He didn't look up when his mother knocked tentatively on his bedroom door. She stood still, watching

171

him. Her arms crossed tightly up against her chest.

"It's okay to have the odd day off, Harry. Have you finished the picture?"

"Yes, Mother."

"You going to ask me about the girls?"

Harry stopped and laid his paintbrush on the desk. "Yes, yes, Mum. How are they?" For the first time in thirty-six hours he felt something.

"I like it best when you call me 'Mum,' drop the 'Mother' thing – yes?"

"Sure, Moth... Mum."

For Harry, the mention of his three sisters opened a channel in his brain. He heard the Outliner talking to him. Telling him what it wanted. He understood. He scrutinised the image emerging on the paper. He had to carry on with all of this. It didn't matter what they wanted.

There was only a small flicker, somewhere in his mind, which balked at their command.

His mother's routine of taking the girls to their grand-mother's house every Thursday, expanded to Tuesdays too. So Tuesdays and Thursdays Harry stayed on the bus for the round trip home. He was into the third week of this routine when the bus driver finally said something. Harry was about to jump off the bus.

"Harry."

He turned his head nonchalantly. "Yeah?"

"If I see you doing this again, I'll be telling your mum – understood? And Harry..." The bus driver leaned over sideways in his seat. "Tell your mum *hi* from Liam – I probably won't see her next week – I'm on a different route."

Harry grunted. He'd had no idea the driver knew his mother. The automatic doors started to close and his head

172

began to thump. The Outliner was inside him. What did he have to do? He knew he had to be at home for at least two days of the week, when his Mother was out for the day.

The bus driver, *Liam*, was going to make it difficult.

"Oh my God, Harry, have you seen the local paper... my God, my God."

Harry was methodically eating cornflakes. Dispassionately, he watched first his mother and then his three sisters who, as usual, were lined up opposite him. He smiled into his bowl. She saw him.

"What the hell is the matter with you?" she said.

"What do you mean?"

"I know you've read it, Harry. Why didn't you say something? For God sakes, he's our local bus driver – my friend."

"Oh, you mean Liam... died... yes, weird isn't it? They have no idea what he died of. Found at the bottom of his garden – shame."

His mother watched him. She looked at the envelope next to his cereal dish. She walked around the table and picked it up. She read it slowly, Harry saw her looking at the postmark; dated the week before.

"An acceptance for your work? Why didn't you tell me?" She ruffled his head with her hand. He pulled away instinctively and saw her wince.

"Nothing to tell – you don't like me doing it..."

"I don't 'not like you doing it'. I'm just worried that you're spending less time on your school work."

"Doesn't matter – I won't need to pass any exams."

She banged the table with her fist. The three girls stared hard at their mother, deciding when to start crying. Their decision came together. High-pitched wails echoed throughout the kitchen. "Harry, I've had enough of you. I can't cope – your dad's away, the girls are a handful... why are you making my life so difficult?" She picked up Eloise and stroked the two heads of her remaining children. Their crying stopped.

"I'm not. It's you who are making your own life difficult." He glanced over at his three sisters. "Would it be better, Mother, if they weren't around?" He gestured towards his siblings.

"What do you mean? What are you implying?"

He remained silent. Maintaining eye contact; daring her. He watched colour rise, beginning at her neck and rapidly moving upwards, covering her sucked in cheeks.

"I'm not implying anything... Mother. You are bothered by what you're actually thinking – isn't that right?"

She exploded. "Get out of my sight, Harry. Go to school, go anywhere, just get out of my kitchen."

Harry left his mother, who had by now placed Eloise back in her chair. She held her head held firmly in shaking hands, leaning heavily on the kitchen table. He didn't go to school; the Outliner was telling him to go to the tree house.

Things were moving on.

Harry didn't need to sleep to be transported to the spaceship which masqueraded as his tree house but neither did he have to climb up to get inside. He stood at the bottom of the beautifully crafted wooden ladders, closed his eyes and waited impatiently for his body to float upwards and then move headlong through the window.

Once inside he became an Outliner himself. Very little of him remained. Only a miniscule part of his brain continued to be human.

The alien merged into the deep shadows of the electric blue light. It would have been exasperated at this stubbornness

174

of the human condition, but it possessed no emotion, absolutely no human sentiment, and was without any empathy for the part of Harry's brain which was attempting to override all that was alien. The alien was though, monitoring this stubborn fragment of Harry's grey matter, trying to decide the viability of the next stage. As the alien filtered and probed Harry's brain, a sensation rippled and spread throughout a tiny part of the alien's own brain. It felt something. An essence of humanity. It perceived the euphoria of a human spirit. The anticipation of creativity.

On the alien planet, many millions of miles away, in a dark recess of another galaxy, there was a sterile and emotionless world where the entire species had lost the ability to reproduce in the womb. It was the maniacal intervention of biologists on that planet that had, over the preceding thousand or so years, wiped out placental growth. The uterus had disappeared along with mundane intelligence. The aliens had scoured the universe for hundreds of years attempting to find a species that retained the biological ability that they themselves had long ago lost, and one which they could study easily. The blue planet known as Earth had been a superb find. The aliens thought it would be easy. But they hadn't banked on the part of the human brain that was so strongly able to resist their scrutiny. The alien in the spaceship made the decision to instruct Harry to bring his three sisters to it. It had to be Harry, their brother. The triplets' minds were too young to be infiltrated by the alien. There was something preventing it from entering the mind of a new human. Harry had to do it for them.

Even in the alien world, across space, and in an adjacent Galaxy, this alien had a Superior. And although emotion was totally absent, the result of failing an assignment as important as this would have deep repercussions.

Prison and death would be an easy option in the alien's world – but the reality of failure for the alien was much worse than either of these human punishments. The alien's fate would be a purgatory which no human yet, in any time, in any culture, or of any religious persuasion, had any conception of. As a fragment of inherited memory pricked at his enormous brain, the alien understood all of this, yet he continued with his revised plan. He pushed himself into a decision, which on a planet as barren as the alien's ordered and manufactured mind, and a few hundred light years from now, would be a decision he might regret. Because the Outliner – it had now adopted Harry's name for itself – had decided to abort its mission.

Harry felt waves of energy penetrating his skull. He sensed the pulses that were being emitted, now constantly, into the neurones of his brain. And then the synapses ceased to transmit altogether. Harry felt almost total take over.

He was now aware of what the Outliner wanted in return for the success it bestowed on him regarding his endeavours to become an artist. The Outliner wanted, needed, his three sisters.

Harry's Outline left the spaceship and once again became a human body. And then Harry returned to the house to find his three identical siblings.

They were sleeping in their beds. His mother was fast asleep in the bedroom across the landing. Harry tiptoed silently into her room and switched off the baby monitor. He then made his way into the girls' room. It was Eloise who woke up first, followed quickly by her two sisters. They whimpered. Their whimpers turned into loud cries. Harry closed his eyes and began to do what he had been asked to do. Slowly he began linking into the minds of his

176

sisters. It was easier than he thought. Almost too easy.

They stopped crying. Harry watched as their bodies, all three of them, began rising from the bed and move, one after the other, towards the open window. And out they went. Harry transported himself outside. He stood and watched the three fragile bodies moving down the garden. The love he had for his sisters manifested itself into a physical reaction inside the part of his brain the Outliner had found difficult to penetrate. Harry sensed the Outliner's release of him.

Knowing its own fate, the alien allowed Harry to return to himself. Perhaps the human would have managed to do this without its help. The alien knew he would be destroyed before the time its Superior would attempt this again. It accepted this outcome. Knew its own fate. And bathed in the tiny human-like emotion.

The grey cells of Harry's brain began to swell. Synapses fired again rapidly, in an enormous attempt to reclaim itself.

The girls stopped moving; they hovered in the air, very near to the tree house. Harry squeezed his eyes shut and managed to take control for just long enough. The girls floated gently to the ground. He gathered all three in his arms and walked back towards the house. He made his way wearily up the stairs and put each child back in her own bed.

In the spaceship a fragment of the alien's mind unwound and it felt Harry's mind leaving. He experienced briefly the human emotion of love; the alien was unable to comprehend it but attempted to conceptualize the nebulous, fleeting part of Harry's brain that was impervious to its advanced techniques.

The alien had failed voluntarily. He anticipated the punishment of both his disobedience, and failure, that waited light years away from now.

The fraction of Harry's brain that eluded the Outliner needed a few more thousand years to be eradicated; the fragment which pertained strongly to the human sense of divinity and moral code. To the part that still clung to the deep belief of God and Omnipotence. The alien pondered. A flicker of something long ago lost continued to manifest inside its advanced brain.

It wouldn't be this Outliner who returned a long time from now. Unknowingly, it would be Harry's descendants who would betray themselves and allow the intervention of the aliens.

This Outliner accepted the concept forming in its head. To allow the human – Harry – to retain the creative powers it had unleashed; powers the alien recognised were inextricably linked to the abstract and inaccessible part of Mankind's brain.

"Harry, what on earth are you doing?" His mum was watching him from the doorway. Harry and Eloise lay peacefully on her bed, where at least half an hour ago, he had changed the baby's nappy.

"Sorry, Mum – I was really relaxed." He placed his baby sister gently in the middle of the bed. "I've just had the strangest daydream – a great idea for a painting, it was a bit surreal, Mum." He smiled at her. "I'll have to do this more often, maybe the girls are my muses…"

She laughed. "Yes, maybe, Harry – come on, time for school. Liam's my friend, but he'll only wait so long for you at the bus stop… And thanks Harry," she said.

"No probs," he replied.

Before he left, Harry ran downstairs and into the garden. A heavy mist had settled and his view was unclear. He glanced at the tree house and the massive trees surrounding it. There was no wind; the trees appeared to be frozen – as they would look in a painting. The ginger tom *meowed* at him; his long back was arched. *Must have a bird in sight.* Harry began to turn around and then hesitated. In the corner of his eye he was sure he saw a flicker of florescent blue light. He squeezed his eyes shut and then opened them again. Maybe there wasn't any blue light, but Harry was almost certain he saw a something move in the tree.

And then nothing. Just stillness.

He smiled to himself and turned towards the house. He'd better not keep Liam waiting.

As Harry walked across the patio he deliberately ignored the strong sensation that he was being watched.

## Julie-Ann Corrigan

Julie-Ann has a degree in History/English, but then went on to become a physiotherapist. She returned to her first love – fiction – in 2008 and instantly became hooked.

Her short stories and articles are published in anthologies and online publications. 2012 has seen her long-listed in a novel opening competition, and her story, *Cliché* was included in the Soho House Anthology. She has recently completed her first novel and is working on her second. As a relatively new writer, she enjoys writing and experimenting in different genres.

She lives in Berkshire, and is married to Steve. They have one literature-mad daughter.

# Virus

It is hard to imagine how, in the solitude of space, it would feel to be returning home after ten years alone searching the universe for signs of new life on distant planets. Ten lonely years spent in the sole company of those celestial bodies visited and the cold inhuman voice of the ship's on-board computer. Would a less than sane man have cracked before the mission reached adolescence? Or would traits of insanity be an essential requirement in the character of anyone drafted for such a mission? Especially as those ten years of searching the void for mankind's universal neighbour finally led to the disheartening discovery that the Earth existed in a ghost town of a galaxy. The mission had resulted in hundreds of planets, moons and asteroids being charted and classified. But one after the other was found to be uninhabited or uninhabitable.

The vast emptiness of space had remained that. Empty. Each planet had proven to be more barren than the last. The further away from the Earth the ship travelled the more hostile the environment became. Subconsciously the search for life ceased well before the mid point of the outward bound mission and the mining of rock samples became the prime motive.

The reward for those ten years cruising from one barren world to another was a hundred thousand tons of rock. Not one new alien life form had been discovered and now all that was left was to go home.

"OK, DOC. Wrap this one up and let's head for home," barked Grant, his instructions sounding their usual hollow self in the emptiness of the ships bridge.

"Initiating planetary orbital breakout procedure,

Commander Grant," replied the toneless voice of Delta-3's on-board computer. "Please confirm destination co-ordinates."

Grant scanned the digital display and accepted the coordinates DOC had provided. He had lost count of how many times he had wished for those co-ordinates over the last two years and now there they were, programmed into the ship's main navigation guidance system. Finally, Earth's co-ordinates were displayed on the screen in full dayglo orange for Grant to see.

"Please ensure you are secured for orbital breakout. Main escape rockets will fire in ninety, nine zero, seconds," the computer informed Grant.

Though Grant had been through this breakout procedure countless times before, the nearer he had got to the end of his mission the more he had begun to have irrational fears that the computer would screw up the calculations and send Delta-3 plummeting into the deadly planet surface below.

"Sixty seconds to orbital breakout," DOC continued oblivious to the growing concern on Grant's face.

"Forty five seconds to orbital breakout. Igniting photon drive."

Grant had soon become annoyed at having to listen to DOC's regimented full count down preceding each orbital breakout. He was sure that after well over a hundred or so breakouts there was no need for it and he longed to be able to reprogram its monotonous tone. Each time he felt the urge to scream at DOC to get on with it but knew that the computer was not programmed to recognise the irritation in his command.

As he checked his seat harness he took solace in the fact that this should be the last time he would have to put up with being slingshot out of yet another god-forsaken

181

barren rock's orbit. He was finally returning home. No more dead worlds. No more void. He was going back to colour and life.

"Fifteen seconds to orbital breakout." DOC trundled on.

"Damn it DOC! You've done it again!" Grant growled to computer. He had noticed that on the last three breakouts DOC had skipped announcing thirty seconds. There had not been any decrease in the time, just that the pause between forty-five and fifteen seemed all the greater because of it.

Grant had run check after check on the control software the first time it happened and could find no fault. The second time he physically counted the time down to prove to himself that the computer was not losing any time.

Grant was slightly perplexed by this development. His main concern was that if the computer were starting to miss out part of the countdown, what else was is likely to 'forget' to do?

"Ten, nine, eight, seven, six – engaging photon drive – four, three, two, one, firing photon drive". DOC trundled on, oblivious to Grant's concerns.

Grant felt the now familiar faint rumbling of the ship's photon drive firing up which then slowly began to build in intensity getting ready to rip the spacecraft away from the gravitational pull of the planet below.

Finally, as the full force of the drive cut in Delta-3 was catapulted back into the darkness of outer space. Grant hated that. It always caught him by surprise, even now after all this time, no matter how he prepared himself for it. He was convinced that now, orbiting every heavenly body he had visited, was the minutest portion of his intestine which had been left behind by that final dramatic explosive wrench. He had come to see it as a form of exchange with the celestial body in question in recompense for the rocks brutally snatched away from its surface.

After fifteen minutes at break neck speed Grant felt the ship begin to slow down.

"Gravitational pull zero. Orbital breakout procedures complete. Photon drives disengaging. Main thrusters engaging. Co-ordinates computed and course set. Co-ordinates identified as Planet Earth. Estimated time of arrival at new destination is six point five years," DOC confirmed.

Grant was relieved that the return journey home was going to be relatively much quicker than the outward one. The ship was programmed to return straight to Earth at optimum speed. The stop-start nature of the outward journey was now history and his next scheduled destination would be Earth.

Satisfied that everything was as it should be, he thumped the safety harness open and climbed out of the command chair. Finally, after ten years of solitude, he was going home.

Grant left the ship's control room and started back to his living quarters pondering the magnitude of his achievements during what he had come to refer to as his Great Quest for Extra-terrestrial life. After all this time all it mounted up to was a big fat zero. He had spent the last ten years of his life searching for something, however small, to indicate that life did exist away from the carbon-based planet he knew as home and he had absolutely nothing to show for it.

This depressing thought prompted a familiar voice to sound off in his head.

*"Hi! It's me again. How do you think they will receive*

*the Messenger of Doom back on Earth when he returns with the bad news from the galactic neighbourhood? Sorry folks, we are on our own. There's no-one out there. You've just wasted ten years of your life searching for something that does not exist. Sixteen if you count the journey home!"*

Unsurprisingly the voice was always that of his ex-wife.

Grant scowled and the voice scurried back to hide amongst the dark, twisted brain cells that it had emerged from.

He had been hearing the voice of his dearly hated ex-wife in his head now for the last six months and each time she reared her ugly voice it reminded him of at least one reason why the return to Earth was not without its drawbacks. However, sixteen years was a long time and who was to say his ex-wife was still around. He had been warned when he had accepted the mission that he would come back to great changes. If she was still there maybe she may have mellowed and forgiven him. Grant shook his head. They had told him that the changes would be great, not miraculous.

He arrived outside his quarters and activated the door. He entered and the door closed automatically behind him. The internal lights slowly sparked into life bathing the room in a low orange glow that steadily built to a bright white glare. He crossed to the drink cabinet and poured himself a large straight scotch.

Here was another reason for going home. His scotch supply was getting dangerously low. He probably had enough to last him five of the six years left of the journey home meaning he would have to ration himself. This was going to be difficult as he had noticed an increase in his scotch intake over the last few months. An increase that, not surprisingly, coincided with the emergence of the nagging voice that now frequented his head. In this respect he could be thankful to DOC who had been programmed to release just the one bottle per ten day period. He was also thankful that so far there had always been some scotch left in the old bottle at the end of each period. However the amount left was slowly beginning to decrease.

Grant kicked off his shoes and stretched out on the padded bench that, along with the bed, table, desk and solitary chair, constituted his furniture.

He was tired. Preparing and executing an orbital breakout always drained him. He drank heavily from the glass. The warm liquid soothed his gullet as it journeyed south into the unknown, an ally to the drowsiness that was now befalling him. He placed the glass on the table beside him. As sleep marched fearlessly onward, he closed his eyes. As he did so, images of the last ten years came creeping stealthily toward him. Images of planets visited, of space, of earth, of life before the Great Quest...

Sleep had refused to be a friend to him recently. Constantly, no doubt brought on by his impending return to Earth, scenes of his life prior to this mission would ricochet through his dreams. Scenes that were predominantly his astronaut training, his first space voyages aboard the NASA Space Shuttle missions to build the space station that would enable the building of the Delta-3 spaceship he now piloted, his selection for the mission and finally leaving Earth behind.

Interspersed with this were the lowlights of his marriage to Kim, his first and only wife and their subsequent demise thanks to Grant's indiscretion with a fellow female astronaut, caught on a NASA videotape for all to see.

These events in his life had raged indiscriminately

through his unconsciousness regularly during the past ten years. They were intermittent at first but gained in regularity over the last twelve months or so. In his saner, wakeful moments, Grant had tried to analyse what their meaning could be. He was undecided as to whether they were the past haunting him or a reminder of what life would probably hold for him in the future. Now as his mission was complete and he headed for home he thought that the latter felt more probable.

His troubled mind finally slinked into the shadows of deep sleep satisfied that its torment was complete.

Grant slept for a full twelve hours. It would be tempting to say 'that night' but night and day had long since mingled into one long expanse of time for Grant. Time no longer held any meaning for him, his only perception of it being through DOC's request for the regular 'daily' report log.

He would have probably slept for another couple of hours if he had not been brought rudely back to reality by the dull pulsing scream of Delta-3's on-board alarm. Grant groggily launched himself from the bench, putting his shins on a collision course with the table, an act that sent his half-empty glass skimming across the floor to shatter on contact with the wall.

"For Christ Sake," Grant grunted rubbing his injured shins to ease the stinging pain now throbbing through them. He grabbed his boots from the floor and, attempting to put them on as he ran, stumbled to the door, crunching through broken glass as he went. The ship's siren gained in intensity the more Grant's consciousness returned. The high pitched wail seemed to reverberate in his temples causing him to cradle his head in his hands. The sour aftertaste of the scotch that lined his mouth gave fuel to the feeling of unrealism.

Exiting the room, his brain was starting to work its way around possible reasons for DOC to sound the alert. At best it was yet more evidence of the computer slipping into malfunction mode and generating a false alarm. At worst, the ship could be about to self destruct or, Grant's fiercest nightmare, shut down completely so condemning him to a silent, floating tomb, millions of miles from home.

Bursting into the control room he finally shook off the ineptitude of sleep, his training bringing him to a fully operational state.

"Specify alert condition," he barked at DOC.

"Long range sensors have detected a large object located within our projected flight path," DOC replied.

Grant was slightly taken aback by this. Being on collision course with another object was not an option that he had considered on his short journey back to the control room. DOC was programmed to detect asteroids, meteors and the like and then to take the necessary evasive action so Grant was puzzled that the computer had needed to sound the alert anyway.

"Identify and quantify detected object," Grant requested.

"Object is located twenty thousand galactic miles from the ship. Preliminary scanning indicates that it is two miles in length and one half mile in width. The object is constructed from a material not listed in any accessible databank." DOC detailed.

"Could the object be any type of meteorite or asteroid?" Grant enquired.

"Negative," DOC returned. "Object does not relate to any known properties associated with any known natural formations of rock or metal based bodies."

"Does the object relate to any known formation detailed on your databanks?" Grant continued.

"Object exhibits certain properties that can be related to data stored." DOC offered.

Grant's pulse quickened and he had a slight tremble in his voice as he asked the next question.

"What object stored in your databanks relates to the unidentified mass?"

"Object detected has properties similar to Delta-3." DOC returned matter-of-factly.

Grant sat back in his seat unaware that he was holding his breath.

Grant stared at the monitor for a full five minutes before regaining a grip on his conscious self. In those five minutes, a myriad of thoughts ran through a part of his brain that had gradually become a dead end during the latter part of the last ten years. That part of his brain known as his imagination. Disappointment after disappointment had slammed shut the door to this alleyway, hinges rusted by the fruitless march through infinity.

But now, a seed of hope had grasped hold of a crowbar and wrenched free that portal, only slowly at first, not wishing to obliterate this new-found hope. Then, with a release of air like that from a long enclosed Egyptian tomb, the door burst open to release long lost dreams of life among the stars.

Grant returned to reality with a start, the need for tangible proof beating back the follies of fantasy. Regaining his control, his mind slipped into procedural mode.

"Highlight properties of unidentified object similar to Delta-3" Grant requested, still feeling a little bemused.

DOC went silent for what seemed like an eternity though Grant knew the computer would be scanning the object before returning its answer. However, he was just about to lose his patience with DOC and repeat the command when the computer fired into life.

"Unidentified object exhibits structural properties similar to Delta-3. It appears to consist of an outer fabricated skin secured to a framework similar in design to Delta-3. Though of an unknown type the object exhibits areas within its core that are conducive to being propulsion units. However, initial analysis concludes that these are inactive and the object is drifting powerless. Scanners detect large cavernous areas similar in design to the holds of Delta-3. Smaller areas of the object relate to the living and functional areas of Delta-3."

DOC finished its brief summation.

Grant pondered this information before asking the next question.

"Compute the likelihood of the object being naturally occurring." He requested.

Doc went silent again but was back with its calculation within seconds.

"Likelihood of object being naturally occurring is less that 1%." DOC continued in its matter of fact way.

Grant computed the meaning of this himself. What DOC was intimating was that the object had a 99% certainty of being man-made. Or in its particular case, alien-made!

"Compute the estimated time of rendezvous with craft". He requested well aware of the assumptions he was already beginning to make.

"Object will be in space walk range in twelve hours, fifteen minutes and twenty three seconds." DOC replied. "Preliminary scan indicates the object is travelling at negligible speed on a trajectory ninety degrees to the flight path of Delta-3".

"Confirm there is no indication of the craft's power source." Grant demanded.

"No power source detected."

Grant allowed himself some thinking time to take stock of the apparent data on offer so far. Here floating in space was an object not dissimilar to the craft he was aboard. Its only motion was probably caused by solar wind. The object was in a position very close to Delta-3's trajectory. If the object was what he thought it might be, then maybe he could be on the verge of fulfilling his mission after all. He cleared his mind and prepared himself for the answer to the next question.

"Does the scan indicate the possibility of any form of life onboard the craft?"

DOC remained silent.

"DOC, confirm last data request," Grant growled, his concern as to the functioning of DOC becoming evermore great.

"Request confirmed. Object appears devoid of any known life form. Preliminary readings indicate that the object is hollow but contains an atmosphere not conducive to sustaining any known terrestrial life."

Grant did not know whether to take this as good news or bad. On one hand, it was bad news that the atmosphere was not suitable for him to breathe without the aid of a spacesuit. The unconscious assumption that he would be going aboard this craft had been made a long time before. The good news was that, though it indicated no sign of known comparable terrestrial life, this did not rule out the possible existence of alien life way beyond the comprehension of even DOC. DOC had been programmed to recognise all types of known life forms, and even to extrapolate life properties to take into account numerous conditions that may occur in space to try and predict how alien life might have developed. But no one on Earth could have predetermined all the types of life that might exist in the universe.

Grant surveyed space out through the forward monitor. Only the stars were visible for now but soon, very soon, a new and interesting object would be coming into view.

"Begin transmission of universal greeting on all frequencies," Grant commanded.

The universal greeting was a message he had DOC transmit each time they approached a new planet or moon. It was an attempt to let any life forms that may exist that the ship came in peace. Until now, Grant had given up on any reply. But this time he was a little more optimistic.

However, after three hours of transmission no reply had been received that he could even vaguely construe as an attempt by any occupants of the craft to communicate with him.

"Continue transmitting at five minute intervals," Grant barked feeling a little frustrated.

If he could not get any response from the craft, then he would have to assume that it was abandoned and go out to it. He turned to leave the command centre. It was time to make ready his spacesuit.

The next nine or so hours seemed to last an eternity to Grant. He had prepared his suit in double quick time and was now staring impatiently at the spacescape in front of him.

At first all he could see were the billions of stars he had been gazing upon for the last ten years. Then, slowly, he was able to focus on one particular bright star that appeared to be growing in size. Slowly, the star became larger and larger until he began to make out the vague shape of the alien craft he was travelling toward.

"Prepare to shut off engines," he ordered DOC.

"Engines ready for shutdown," DOC replied.

"Commence engine shutdown," Grant commanded.

His calm exterior did not betray the excitement that was beginning to build inside him. However, again his years of disciplined training kept him cool.

"Engine shutdown commenced," DOC answered and with that, Grant felt the sudden deceleration as his body gently pulled forward. As he steadied himself, DOC reported back that the engines had been shutdown and the breaking sequence had been started which would bring the ship to a complete standstill.

"Bring Delta-3 within one thousand metres of the craft and then engage trickle thrusters to match the drift of the craft," Grant commanded.

DOC confirmed the order had been carried out.

Grant then asked DOC for an up to date status report on the alien object that now filled his forward screen. Delta-3 was now close enough to the craft for Doc to carry out a more detailed scan.

"The object does not appear to be generating any power. Still no known lifeforms detected. There is still no response to the greeting message transmission."

"Calculate how long it would take to reach the object using the space jet". This was a device he attached to his spacesuit when he needed to manoeuvre about space if and when he embarked on one of his rare space walks.

"Five minutes and twenty seconds," came DOC's reply.

*Good,* thought Grant. His space suit carried enough oxygen for him to operate for two hours maximum. He would be able to hold Delta-3 in this position and still have ample time to get to the alien craft, have a good look around it and then return to his ship before the oxygen ran out.

"Prepare airlock five," Grant barked and before DOC could confirm, he was striding out of the control room.

Twenty minutes later he was suited up and exiting the airlock. Space walks always gave him a buzz. However, as he emerged from airlock five he felt an adrenaline rush that left him slightly giddy with excitement. From inside Delta-3, the alien craft looked impressive enough on the monitor. But now, as he emerged from the airlock into the vulnerability of space, it looked awesome.

Back on Earth, he had heard all the tales of extra terrestrial craft being spotted flashing through the atmosphere. All shapes and sizes had been reported from cylindrical cigar shapes to spherical balls of light in the sky. But no description he had come across of those craft did justice to the sight that now lay in front of him.

What struck Grant was the shape of the alien craft. It was triangular in shape with what looked like rows of lights along each edge. The alien craft was at least twice the size of Delta-3. However, true to DOC's information about there being no power source, these lights were not illuminated.

The hull of the craft looked as if it had endured a number of meteor strikes. It was pitted with craters that had dented whatever material the craft had been made of. It was obvious that this material was able to endure substantial hits due to the size of the dents on the surface of the craft. However, there were two or three areas where the impact had been of sufficient force to puncture the outer skin. It gave Grant the impression of a great slain beast that had had chunks of its flesh ripped away by some vociferous galactic carnivore.

Grant wondered if the damage he was seeing had been the cause of the craft's seeming demise, or whether it had been wreaked upon the ship after some other calamity. Whichever was the correct scenario, Grant's gut feeling was that the craft was a wreck and had been for some time.

As he got closer to the craft, Grant could see that at least two of the puncture wounds seemed large enough to allow him access inside. This was fortuitous as he realised that he had not given much thought beforehand as to how he was to gain access to the craft. If not for the gaping wounds on the side of the craft, how would he have made his entry? He thought about this for a second and then tossed the problem overboard. There was no point in cluttering his mind with redundant thoughts.

He weighed up the two proposed entry points. There was not a great deal of difference between them. He mentally tossed a coin in his mind and naturally chose the nearest.

He manoeuvred the spacejet to the hole and stopped for a second gazing into the darkness of the craft's interior. He switched on his helmet torch and scanned around. From the limited view that he had the hole seemed to enter into a large, high ceiling room that looked like it could have been one of the cargo holds identified by DOC.

Grant took a deep breath and crawled in.

As he stepped in Grant marvelled at the size of the hold. It reminded him of the first time he had stepped inside Delta-3's cargo bay, filled so far with the unexciting fruits of his journey, before his mission started. That had been well lit and the sheer size of it had left him awestruck. However, even in the dim light of his helmet torch he could tell that this hold must have been at least four or five times as big. This would make it at least two-thirds the length of the craft.

Grant stood just inside the craft and scanned around. He could see the second damage hole to the right of him.

The stars shining outside were in stark contrast to the pitch-black void within the hold.

From what he could make out with his limited vision, the hold was virtually empty. His first thoughts were that perhaps the craft had been disabled not long into its flight. The holes in the side of the craft were of reasonable size and there certainly would have been a degree of explosive decompression when whatever hit it punched its way in. But from what he could see, there did not seem to be any evidence of wreckage of any cargo the craft could have been carrying as it was wrenched into space from inside.

It also puzzled him that there was no evidence of any meteors within the hold. Logic dictated that if the ship had been punctured by such an object, there would at least be some debris inside the craft.

With this thought in mind, Grant slowly paced through the hold. He produced a second, handheld torch from a pocket on the outside of his left space suit leg. This torch was of considerably greater power than the one sitting on top of his helmet. He fumbled for its switch which was not an easy manoeuvre considering the size of the switch compared to the bulkiness of the fingers on his gloves. However, he managed to switch the torch on and the cargo hold was lit up at least ten times brighter than with the helmet torch alone.

In the increased light, Grant could see the cargo hold more clearly. To the right about four or five hundred metres away, he could see what he thought must have been the entrance to the hold from the main craft. Behind him he had the wound-like hole he had come through. To his left, all he could see after his torchlight had ended was the darkness of the hold.

But what he saw fifty metres in front of him made his mouth drop open. He stood there for at least two minutes hardly able to comprehend the sight that was now illuminated before him.

There, in rows about thirty deep, as many wide, and twice as many high, were transparent pods. Each pod was of the same shape and size, two metres long, one metre wide and one metre high. They appeared to be made of a Perspex-type material and even from the distance he was away from them; he could see that each one contained what appeared to be a body.

Grant composed himself and slowly walked over to the pods stopping about a metre away from the first bank of them. They were supported on frames not dissimilar to the shelving Grant was familiar with back in the hold of Delta-3. The skeletal framework was approximately twenty centimetres squared with the pods directly attached to it. Each pod appeared to have four clips, one at each corner, which secured it to the framework.

Grant moved to the nearest pod and gazed dumbfound at the body inside hardly believing that he was actually looking down at the outline of an alien creature.

The being inside was unlike any other creature he had ever seen. Its body was unclothed and completely hairless. Its skin was dark brown and smooth with a mottled texture that Grant thought looked like the leather used for furniture back on Earth.

He could see no genitalia on the body so wondered if the species had different sexes and if so how could it be determined whether the creature was male or female. Its torso was about a metre long and quite plump. It reminded Grant of a sea lion he had once seen in one of the zoos he had visited on Earth. On either side of it, emerging about half way down were tentacles covered in sucker-like pads. He could see no discernible hands and there appeared to be no joints connecting the appendages to the body. They

196

seemed to be growing out of the side of the alien like a branch sprouting from a tree.

The creature's distinctive triangular head was connected to its body by a short, thick stump. Its wide forehead angled down to a pointed chin like feature that hung down over the creature's chest area.

The creature did not have a face in the traditional human sense. There were no contours visible leaving the face completely flat. It appeared to have two slits in a position where eyes could have been located, a slit in the region of a nose and a slit either side the head which could have acted as ears. However, Grant knew he was making assumptions. He was well aware that he should be the last person to pronounce himself expert on alien anatomy. These slits reminded him of fish gills and he wondered if the function of some of them may be similar. He also noticed that each of the slits had what looked like green slimy mucus oozing from them.

The main feature of the alien's face was the large hole that sat centrally and just below what he now thought of as the nasal gill. It was wide open exposing a double row of teeth with serrated edges which look capable of ripping through flesh with no problem at all. Grant shivered at the thought of coming face to face with one of these creatures when it was alive.

The lower half of the creature consisted of what appeared to be a single stump like leg about seventy centimetres long. It was thick and just like the tentacle arms did not seem to contain any joints as Grant knew them. He thought it looked very much like an elephant's leg and he was curious as to how this creature would have moved about using this single appendage.

Grant stood there amazed. He could not believe that he had finally discovered proof of alien life outside of Earth and the significance that his mission had now taken on. He spent time moving around the hanger checking on the other pods that were held there and he found that they all contained similar creatures that only differed in size and skin colouring.

Grant checked his air supply monitor and to his amazement saw that it was now showing below half full. He had lost track of time and could not believe he had been out of Delta-3 for over an hour. His priority now was to work out how to detach one of the pods, take it back to his ship with him so he could get a clearer look at the body and get it stored for the journey back to Earth.

He felt around the clips that held the pod to the frame and discovered that they unfastened quite easily. He undid all four and gently nudged the pod free. It floated away with ease and Grant had to grab it to stop it gliding off on its own. He positioned himself behind it and began to push it toward the gaping hole through which he had entered the craft.

Grant manoeuvred the pod toward the hole which, with the luxury of there being no gravity, he found to be an exertion free task. He brought it to a halt a metre or so away from the hole. He wanted to be able to exit the ship first and then pull the pod out so that he could maintain control of it. He was concerned that should he push it out, he may lose grip and send it sailing off into the void. Having got it this far he did not want to lose it. His oxygen supply was beginning to run low and if he had to go back inside the alien craft to retrieve another pod then he would first have to return to his ship to replace his air supply.

His sole concentration now was set on getting the pod safely stored away in the hold of his ship. Once this had been achieved he then planned to return and retrieve at least three more of the alien bodies before he carried on home.

He stepped around the pod and, with his back virtually through the hole, pulled the pod toward him. When he was sure that he would be able to reach the pod from outside the craft he slowly stepped backwards into the void. Once more he was in the starry void and floating alongside the impressive alien craft.

Using the thrusters on the space jet to turn him he positioned himself so that he was at ninety degrees to the hull of the craft and then set them so that they would maintain him in this position. When he was sure he was he in position he placed both gloved hands onto the pod and began to pull it alongside him and out of the alien ship. Once he had extracted it from the ship he glided it to a position where he could slip behind it and then, using the thrusters, gradually pushed it across the emptiness to his own ship before bringing it to a stop just short of the air lock.

Gently he rounded the pod until he reached the outer shell of the air lock door. He pulled the locking leaver and with a hiss of compressed air the door glided smoothly inward and upward.

Grant turned back to the pod and then with great care guided it into the air lock. Once it was inside he fired his thrusters and followed it in expertly stopping himself just inside the ship at the large red button used for closing the air lock door. He reached out and pushed it. The air lock door slid back down and outward, sealing him in from the vacuum outside. Twenty seconds later the room started to depressurise and fill with breathable air. Grant watched the gauge next to the button move steadily up from red to green indicating that the room was now able to sustain him without him having to depend upon his artificial air supply. He moved unsteadily toward the far side of the air lock to where the door to the main ship was located. After being in the weightlessness of space he always found it took him a little time to get his gravity legs back again.

Grant located the green button next to the internal door and pushed it. The door slid to the side and allowed him entrance into the main ship. When the ship was designed it was decided that the buttons controlling the entrance to the air lock from the ship and exit into space should not only be coloured differently but also located as far apart from each other as possible. This was to ensure there was no fatal mix up in pushing the buttons at the wrong time which could cause a catastrophic blow out to the ship.

Grant re-entered Delta-3 and removed his helmet. He breathed in the sterile air that always tasted a little bitter after the sweet mixture of pure oxygen used during his space walks. However, the doctored air had kept him germ free over the last ten years and he had never once suffered any cold symptoms or bug of any kind.

He placed his helmet on the wall rack that ran along one side of the changing room and then did likewise with the jet pack and air tank he carried on his back. He hooked the air tank feeder pipe into a nozzle on the wall and pushed a blue button next to it. Grant heard the low hiss of the oxygen mixture being fed into the air tank so replenishing it. When he was ready to return to the alien ship he would now have to pick up a new pack as they 'took a good twenty four hours to refill fully.

Grant turned his thoughts to the problem of transporting the pod from the air lock to the cargo bay. In getting it across from the alien ship he had been able to use the lack of gravity to his advantage. Now, back on the ship, he had lost this. In truth, he was not even sure how much the pod weighed. Even if he was able to lift it, it was far too bulky to be able to pick it up and carry it through the ship. He did not want to risk dropping it and disturbing the precious cargo held within.

Grant scratched his chin while he calculated his options. He then remembered there was a gurney in the cargo hold of the ship which he had used for transporting rocks. He took a brisk walk down to the hold and ten minutes later he was wheeling the gurney through the air lock door and lining it up next to the pod.

He positioned himself at the mid point of the pod and then, bending his knees he crouched down and attempted to tilt it enough to slide his hands underneath it. To his surprise he found that he could raise it quite easily and soon had it cradled on his forearms. Taking a deep breath he stood up and then slid the pod onto the gurney.

Pleased with his efforts so far he took time to have another look into the pod at the alien guest he now had on board. Under the bright light of the air lock room he could see the body much clearer. Still not believing what had transpired over the last few hours he started to wheel the gurney and its passenger down the corridor to the cargo hold.

Grant spent the next eight hours travelling to and from the alien space craft managing to transfer a further three bodies to Delta-3's cargo hold. He had settled on retrieving five of the alien creatures before he continued on his journey home.

On the fifth sortie he decided to see if he could get into the main part of the ship and take a look around inside it. He made his way to what he surmised to be the entrance to the inner ship. However, despite his best endeavours he could not work out how to open the door and resigned himself to finding alternative access to the main ship. His initial thoughts were that once he had finished transferring the bodies across to Delta-3 he would take a space walk around the exterior of the alien craft and see if there were any further damaged areas from which he could gain access.

He returned to the pods, selected his final specimen and transported it back to Delta-3. Just as he had stepped out of his space suit and was preparing to move the pod down to the cargo hold the ship's alarm started to sound off again.

Grant hit the intercom button on the wall.

"Status report," he growled into the mouth piece.

"Scanners detect incoming objects on direct collision course with Delta-3" DOC returned without emotion.

"Time to impact?" Grant queried.

"Five minutes and thirty seconds," Doc answered.

"Initiate evasive action," Grant barked out.

The intercom remained silent. Grant punched the button again.

"Confirm last directive," he fired at DOC.

"Five minutes and thirty seconds," DOC repeated.

Grant stared at the wall before punching the button for a third time.

"Initiate evasive action," Grant spoke slowly and clearly.

"Five minutes and thirty seconds," DOC's dull tone insisted.

Grant was just thinking that DOC was malfunctioning good and proper this time when the meteor struck Delta-3's hull.

Grant grabbed the gurney and just managed to prevent it from tipping over.

"Taking evasive action," DOC echoed calmly across the room.

The impact of the meteor seemed to have jolted DOC into action and Grant felt the ship's proton engage. Delta-3 turned sharply to the left and Grant was flung off his feet. As he tried to keep upright he grabbed at the gurney but his bodyweight had already passed its centre of gravity and Grant continued on toward the floor. The gurney followed suit and toppled over causing the pod to crash side on into the floor. The casing smashed and the alien body sprawled onto the floor amidst an out rush of foul smelling air. Grant placed his hand over his mouth and nose concerned about what he may be breathing in. However he was not quick enough and his lungs filled with the putrid gas that had been released. He felt the room spin and then passed out.

Grant gradually came around still tasting the foul air in his mouth. He felt nauseous and his head felt as if it were being crushed between two of the rocks he had been meticulously collecting.

The alien body was still where it had landed but Grant could see that the green mucus that had been oozing from each of the slits on the body was now pooling around it. He could not believe the amount of mucus there now seemed to be.

He felt the need to vomit and tried to sit up but could not. Lying on his stomach he turned his head to the side as he retched up the same foul mucus that the alien body was now lying in.

He felt the mucus start oozing from his nose and tried again to get up but his body would not respond. He was paralysed and he found it increasingly difficult to breathe. He could feel his lungs beginning to fill with the sticky liquid and slowly began to lose consciousness again. The room began to grow dark and Grant's body gave a final jolt as the alien virus extinguished his life.

Delta-3 remained stationary four thousand metres from the alien craft. DOC had manoeuvred it a safe distance away from the meteor shower and had managed to save it from any serious damage.

The ship remained silent while DOC awaited its next command unaware that Commander Grant's days of issuing orders were over.

So DOC waited and waited. After a year of waiting and receiving no command, its fail safe programme kicked into life directing DOC to access the coordinates for Earth and take Delta-3 home.

**Phil Hodgkiss**

Phil Hodgkiss is a 49 year old Local Government Officer who writes in his spare time. Having built up a collection of short stories, Phil has also completed his first novel – *Gulls*. With a strong interest in horror, Phil enjoys writing stories that chill.

For more information visit
https://sites.google.com/sites/philswriting/home

# Index of Authors

# Other Publications by Bridge House

## On This Day

### *edited by Debz Hobbs-Wyatt and Gill James*

Everyone remembers what they were doing when the shocking
news broke: when Kennedy was shot, when Princess Diana
died and when the first plane crashed into the World Trade
Centre on 9/11. Yet everyday lives continued with their own
ups and downs. This collection shows us some of those possible stories and how they are gently connected with the day's
world shattering event.

A percentage of the author royalties will be donated to International Rescue Training Centre Wales (IRTCW), who provide
search and rescue dogs to the Emergency services.

Order from www.bridgehousepublishing.co.uk

Paperback: ISBN 978-1-907335-21-1
eBook: ISBN 978-1-907335-22-8

# Voices of Angels

## *edited by Debz Hobbs-Wyatt*

Do you believe in angels? This collection of fictional short stories explores encounters with angels – in whatever form they take. Some stories are sad, some are funny; all will touch you. The collection includes a new story by Laura Wilkinson.

The foreword is written by TV and Radio Presenter, Gloria Hunniford, and for every copy sold a donation will be made to her cancer charity: The Caron Keating Foundation – set up in her daughter's memory.

Order from www.bridgehousepublishing.co.uk

Paperback: ISBN 978-1-907335-15-0
eBook: ISBN 978-1-907335-18-1

## *BloodMining*

### *by Laura WIlkinson*

Megan Evens appears to have it all: brains, beauty, a successful career as a foreign correspondent. But deep down she is
lonely and rootless. Pregnant, craving love but unable to trust
after the destructive affair with her baby's father she returns to
the security of her birthplace in Wales.

When Megan's son is later diagnosed with a terminal condition, a degenerative, hereditary disease, everything she
believed to be true about her origins is thrown into question.
To save her son Megan must unearth the truth; she must
excavate family history and memory. Enlisting the help of
former colleague Jack North, a man with a secret of his own,
Megan embarks on a journey of self discovery and into the
heart of what it means to be a parent.

"Lean, lyrical, topical and emotionally gripping. This book is
about the issues that we care about most – with a twist. Read it
and pass on the word!"
*Yvonne Roberts, award-winning journalist and author*

Order from www.bridgehousepublishing.co.uk

Paperback: ISBN 978-1-907335-14-3
eBook: ISBN 978-1-907335-16-7